Santa's Secret

New York Times and *USA Today* Bestselling Author
HEIDI MCLAUGHLIN

SANTA'S SECRET
HEIDI MCLAUGHLIN
© 2017

COVER DESIGN: Letitia Hasser ~ RBA Designs.
EDITING: Kellie Montgomery

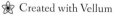 Created with Vellum

Merry Christmas & Happy New Year

ONE

DELANEY

"*A*nd that's a wrap! Great job everyone." The director's joyful yell to end production puts a huge smile on my face. Back-to-back-to-back filming is not my idea of a good time, but it's how my schedule worked out, and I couldn't be happier to have a few months off before my next project starts.

"Wait up, Delaney." I turn to find my co-star, Everett Bowman, jogging after me. Although, it's not really jogging, more like a fast strut that results in the extras on set ogling his backside. Secretly I think he loves every second of the attention he gets, while I couldn't careless since I know about his off-set antics. I believe he's had more girlfriends than I have underwear. "A few of us are heading to Chateau for drinks..." he cocks his head to the side as if I'm supposed to read between the lines.

"Can't, but thanks for the offer."

"Ah, c'mon, it'll be fun."

I smile and shake my head. "Trey and I are heading to Cancun for the holidays. I need to get home and pack."

Everett steps closer and leans into me, kissing me lightly on my cheek. "Well, have a good time and a Merry Christmas. See ya when you get back." He doesn't wait for me to respond or even wish him Merry Christmas before he heads to the group of people waiting for him.

With a little more pep in my step than usual, I work quickly to gather my things from the dressing room, knowing my personal assistant will pack everything else and make sure it's all delivered to me. There are a few things I don't want to live without, though, like the black velvet dress I wore for one of my scenes. It fit me like a glove, and I begged production to let me have it. It isn't uncommon for actors to take clothes from the set, although frowned upon.

Outside, the car service is waiting for me; although normally I have my bodyguard Calvin drive me everywhere. The production company was insistent they provide transportation allowing Calvin to have some much needed and well deserved time off while I'm working. I've had the same driver through the duration of filming and am sad this will be our last drive together and hope that we'll work with each other again soon. I hand him a card as soon as I reach the door. "Merry Christmas, Bill."

"Thank you, Miss Delaney. Merry Christmas to you." He nods and smiles, waiting for me to get into the backseat. Once the door closes, it's only a matter of seconds before we're driving away from the set.

With the privacy window down, we chat about the holidays and what our plans are. Bill mentioned he's looking forward to enjoying a few days off with his grandchildren. He says their laughter keeps him young. I can easily imagine my mother saying the same thing, although she'll have to wait for my brother, Dominic, to have children because I don't see them in my future, at least not in the next five years or so.

I ask him to drop me off at the park where the Christmas displays are set up. As much as I love living in Los Angeles, I miss the snow of Vermont. It's during this time that I long for home and the smell of cinnamon, hot chocolate and the sound of blades cutting through freshly groomed ice.

When Trey suggested we go away for Christmas, I thought it would be a good time for him to come back home with me to meet my family, but he wasn't keen on that idea. I get it; we've only been together for six months, and he's right, it's too soon, whether he's said those words or not.

Still, I miss Ramona Falls, the town I grew up in, and how everyone is overly cheery during the holidays. Of course, with my father as the mayor, I don't think they're given much chance not to be. Every year, my father makes a huge production out of the tree lighting ceremony. My parents get invited to every party, and they rarely miss one. My dad also hires the best Santa there is to give presents to the children during the police officers' party and makes sure there's a team of reindeer on standby if Santa's team can't get the job done. When I was a teen, my dad made Ramona Falls magical.

A few of the storefronts along the park have their decorations up for the holidays. I stop and gaze into the windows, admiring each display before stepping into the park's Winter Wonderland.

The decorations vary throughout each section of the park, everything from Santa's workshop to Mrs. Claus' bakery. Children run about, laughing and singing carols, while their parents chase them. I find myself standing under the snow machine, looking up as the artificial snow hits my face, only to melt instantly. It's unseasonably warm right now, which makes it hard to get into the winter season.

My phone rings, disrupting me from enjoying the snowfall. "Hello, Mom."

"Oh, Delaney, I'm not interrupting you, am I?" She asks the same thing every time I answer the phone. At first, it used to annoy me, but I secretly love that she's concerned.

"Not at all, Mom. I finished early, and now I'm walking through the park, enjoying the decorations and, right now, am standing under the snow machine."

"Are you wearing a hat?"

I laugh. "Nope."

"Well, you'll catch your death."

"It's eighty degrees out," I tell her. "I think I'll be okay."

Mom sighs. "I wish you were coming home. It's been too long."

"I'm sorry, it's just..."

"I know, Delaney. You're in love."

A smile spreads across my face. I am in love, or at least I think I am. Trey Baker has swept me off my feet with his boyish charm and handsome looks. His blonde hair and blue eyes caught my attention while we were filming a movie last year, but it wasn't until this year when we crossed paths again on another set that the sparks flew. We've been inseparable since, well, as far as Hollywood couples can be. We're both tied up with movies, but thankfully our shoots have been local, so we're able to see each other at night or first thing in the morning, depending on our schedules.

"I'll be home soon. I promise."

"Well, it may be sooner than you think because I think Dom is going to propose to Eileen. You know he'll want his sister in the wedding."

"Eek!" I stomp my feet lightly on the ground out of excitement. A few people turn and look at me with funny expressions on their faces, but I don't care. "Are you serious?"

"Well, you know how the gossip mill is."

"For which you're the President. Mom, please tell me you're not spreading rumors and pushing Dominic into proposing."

"What?" Her voice is high-pitched, sounding as if she's shocked. "I would never."

I roll my eyes and turn my back on the lady across from me who has her phone pointed in my direction. I figured under the cloak of darkness I'd be able to wander around without calling much attention to myself, but I was wrong. I'm given no choice but to head toward the line of waiting taxis, ending my night early.

"Are you still there, Delaney?"

"I am, sorry. I'm just trying to dodge someone trying to take a picture."

"See if you come home to Ramona, you wouldn't have these problems. Instead, I'm going to see pictures of my scantily clad daughter basking under the Tuscan sun."

"It's Cancun, and you're jealous."

"I am. I admit it. Anyway, I'll expect a phone call while you're gone."

"I will. I'll call you before I leave. Love you," I say as I open the back door of the cab. I hang up and give the driver my address, watching as the park, and all its magic fades into the distance.

By the time the cab pulls into the parking lot of my condo, I'm exhausted and hungry. I completely forgot to get food while I was out. After paying the driver, I pull my phone out and scroll through the delivery apps, finally deciding on Chinese.

"Trey?" I call out as I open the door. I turn on the lights, the stark white of my home greeting me. It lacks color and life. I bought this place right before I started working on my third to last movie and haven't had time to decorate it yet. Nor have I put up a tree or any other holiday decorations. Even the paintings I've ordered still sit wrapped in the packaging because I haven't had time to hang them up. And neither has Trey. Not that this is his place, but he's been spending time here the past few months.

His bag sits on my bed, filled with clothes. I can't keep the smile off my face. Tomorrow night, we'll be in paradise sipping on cocktails, dancing to native music and sleeping in. The resort caters to celebrities, promising us complete privacy with a private beach not far from our bungalow. The resort staff planned every detail of our trip from our yacht rental to our spa days. We both need this after our hectic schedules.

While I wait for dinner to arrive, I start pulling out my clothes, remembering the dress I stuffed into my bag. I lay that out, fearful of the wrinkles that might set into the fabric. We don't have fancy dinner plans, but I figure I'll bring it just in case. A girl can never be too prepared.

I search my bag for my phone, pulling it out to see if Trey has texted. Nothing. I type one out to him, letting him know I'm home and that I've ordered dinner.

Trey: Be there soon, honey!

My heart flutters at his term of affection in his reply. He's my first serious boyfriend... well since forever, really. Sure, I've dated since coming to Hollywood, but nothing ever took off. Being an actor or actress and trying to date really does take much more effort than any other relationship. We work odd hours, travel all the time, live out of suitcases and use video chat to see our significant others. It takes someone special to understand our jobs.

When I first moved here, the first piece of dating advice I was given was don't date within the industry. That made it a bit harder, but I stayed away from actors. Instead, I dated musicians, people who worked on film sets, guys from different agencies, you name it; if they're in the "movies" I've probably spent a month or so of my life with them, only to have them break-up with me because I'm never free. I thought I would be alone until I met Trey.

Trey has made everything different. While we still have to schedule a time to see each other, it's become like a game for us. When I bought my condominium, I didn't hesitate to give him a key, assuring both of us that he's more than welcome. Honestly, there's nothing that makes me happier than when I come home after a long day on set and find him fast asleep in my bed.

The doorbell rings and I rush to answer it. The local Chinese place is notorious for ringing once and leaving. I swing the door open and catch my breath. "Good, you're still here." The delivery driver rolls his eyes and hands me the slip of paper to sign. The smell of the food has my stomach growling. I don't know if I'll be able to wait for Trey to get here. "Thanks," I say as I smile at him. The young kid hands me the bag of food and stalks away without a single word. "Merry Christmas," I yell out, but he says nothing in return.

"Where's your spirit?" I ask as I close the door, only to remember that I have none according to the lack of decorations. "Next year," I mutter, walking into the kitchen. "Next year, I'm going to decorate and have a party."

The thought of a party has me checking my film schedule for next year. I block off the weekend before the twenty-fifth and add "party" to that Saturday. I'm going to be festive next year if it kills me.

TWO

AIDEN

*T*he alarm on my bedside table goes off. I let it beep while I stare up at the ceiling. "Another day," I say to my empty room before shutting it off. Throwing the covers back, my feet touch the somewhat cold floor. The threadbare carpet needs replacing, among other things. It's on the long list of things I need to do to upgrade this house.

Heather and I bought this place because of the yard. We wanted to give Holly a yard to play in that was safe, and where she could create her own adventures. Also, the land afforded us a place to build a larger garage to store our sixty-five Ford Mustang and a bay for me to tinker with another car. We put the inside of the house on hold, for what seems like forever now.

My bed creaks as I push off it to stand. I stretch and do the yoga poses my physical therapist suggested after I hurt my back on the job. Of course, I only do them for a few minutes and not the thirty that was recommended, but they're done nonetheless.

In the hall, the faint sound of Christmas music plays

from Holly's room. I knock lightly on her door and hear her scramble to get out of bed. As she has gotten older, we've set rules about personal and private space. She needs it, and so do I, but I have reserved the right to bust in without a warrant if I so choose.

"Morning, Daddy." Her toothless smile beams up at me. She's my life, and the reason I get up in the morning. Without her, I don't know where I'd be. I take in her attire. Thermal pants, a sweater, socks and there's a nightgown somewhere because I can see the bottom hanging down.

My house is cold, and weatherizing it was and has been at the top of my list, but there's always something that pushes it down. Of course, the big ticket item is my living room. It lacks flooring. I made the mistake of tearing up what was there, thinking I had the money to put down new hardwood. Who knew one simple mistake in the checkbook can change everything? Not to mention the furnace went out and replacing it was a must, which honestly defeats the purpose if my windows and doors have drafts.

"Good morning, punky. Are you ready for breakfast?" She nods and reaches for my hand. This has been our routine for almost two years. It started when she was five, and I dread the day it stops because I look forward to this moment each morning.

Our kitchen is probably the nicest room in the house. It was remodeled before we purchased and thankfully doesn't need to be touched, although there are features I'd like to change, like the color of the cabinets and the flooring. Someday. That is what I tell myself every day. Someday I'll have the money to fix each project.

Holly climbs up onto one of the bar stools at the end of the island and starts fiddling with some kid meal toy she got when she was with my sister yesterday. If it weren't for

Meredith, I don't know how I'd be able to do half the stuff I do now, like maintaining a full-time job. As is, I've had to ask for special consideration so I can be off by five most nights, but I try to volunteer for overtime as much as I can because we need the money. Not that Holly would ever know. Anything she asks for, I do what I can to get it for her.

"What do you want for breakfast?" I ask as I open the cupboard. Her options are limited, and she knows this. Still, she pretends to think.

"Toast and cereal."

"You got it." On Sunday, after church, we'll go to my parents for brunch but always stay until dinner. A home-cooked meal with my parents beats the boxed dinner I'd end up making. I repeat my mantra as I pour her cereal and her slice of bread toasts, and as I make our lunches for the day. Once the toaster pops, I pour the milk, so her breakfast isn't soggy. "Here ya go."

Holly smiles. "Thanks, Daddy."

While Holly eats, I get ready for work, swapping out my flannel pajama pants for sweats and a t-shirt and throw on a hoodie to keep me warm. Everything I need for work is at the station, in my locker, along with my service weapon. I have an off-duty piece, but since I rarely leave Ramona Falls and our crime rate is very low, I rarely carry it and keep it locked up, so Holly doesn't come across it.

Holly yells that she's done and I ask her to meet me in the bathroom. I try not to hover, but want to make sure she's brushing her teeth properly, so I make it a race. She has yet to figure out that we're racing against nothing because we both brush until the egg timer goes off, yet she wins each and every time. I know one of these days she's going to call me out for it. I just hope it's not anytime soon.

Never in my life did I picture myself as a single dad.

I'm standing behind Holly, watching as she struggles to put her hair in a ponytail. I wish I had learned this from her mother before she left. She took the time to master the smallest details when it comes to raising a daughter, but I didn't.

"Do you want me to help? I saw a video on the web the other day of a dad who used the vacuum to suck his daughter's hair up so he could put the elastic band on it."

Holly calmly sets her brush down and eyes me through the mirror. "You will not use that machine on my hair."

I shrug and continue to watch her, wishing I could be useful. I've thought about asking my sister to take Holly, to let her live with her during the week because I believe it would be better, but I can't bring myself to broach the subject. Honestly, I don't know what I'd do without her around every night.

"There, all done?"

"Are you sure?"

She looks at me again, waiting for me to tell her where she's missed a piece. "Would you like me to braid your hair?" It's the only thing I know how to do. I taught myself by practicing with my shoelaces.

Holly shakes her head and rips the elastic band from her hair, pulling a few strands out. Tears start to form in her eyes. I rest my hand on top of hers and reach for the hairbrush with the other. At first, she shies away, but I keep at it, until her long blonde hair is smooth down her back, and I can gather it at the base of her neck. It's the best I can do for now.

"Aunt Mere can put it up when you see her this morning."

"I like it this way," she says, turning her head from side to side, looking at my sorry excuse for a ponytail. I know she does this to appease me, and I hate it. I want things to be different for her, better.

Meredith, my sister, says I need to get back into the dating world. As luck would have it, she has the best person in mind. In fact, my entire family thinks I should ask Shelby Whittensby out on a date, propose and marry her by the end of the night. I know they want what's best for Holly and me, but I'm not sure Shelby is the answer.

Holly and I grab our lunches and walk to our garage through our breezeway. I've thought about closing this part in to make my bedroom bigger, but it's so far down the list of things I need to accomplish, I can't imagine it'll ever happen, at least not in this lifetime. My biggest fear is I'm going to grow old and die in this house.

Holly goes around to her side of the truck, while I open the garage door. It's ancient and rickety but keeps the snow out. It seems that another few inches fell while we were sleeping last night. I should've set my alarm a few minutes earlier or at least gotten up to look when I woke.

After backing out, I get out and close the garage door. Inside the cab, Holly has changed the station to Christmas music. I groan internally as she starts rattling off her wish list. There are times when I want to tell her Santa's broke, but I refuse to dampen the magic for her.

"When do you think we can get our Christmas tree?"

"Probably this weekend. Maybe we'll go after church."

Holly doesn't say anything; she just nods and continues to stare out the window while she sings along to the radio. "It'll be fun when our living room is done, and we can put the tree in front of the big window. Won't it, Daddy?"

"Mhm. Hopefully next year, but we can still put our tree there," I tell Holly, although unless I win the lottery, it's not likely. I still have mounds of medical bills to pay off that my insurance didn't cover. I think I'm on a payment plan that ends when Holly graduates high school. And that's if nothing happens to either of us from now until then.

I pull into the drop-off and immediately notice my sister talking to Shelby. I groan and throw my truck into drive, praying the two women stay where they are. "I'll pick you up from Aunt Mere's when I'm done."

"Yes, I know. And you'll call if you're going to be late?"

"Or Eileen will." Eileen is our dispatch secretary or better known as the department's work wife. "Love you, punky."

"Love you too." Holly climbs out of my truck and heads toward her group of friends. This year she deemed it unnecessary to give me a kiss goodbye. I pretend like it doesn't bother me, but deep down it does. The first few weeks of school I found myself tearing up as I drove away, wondering how things changed so quickly.

Before I can pull away, my sister waves me down. Hot on her heels is Shelby, with a sunny smile. I wish I could bring myself to ask her out, but I can't. I don't know if it's because she's like Heather, involved in the school and every community event or if it's because I'm just not ready.

"Hey, Mere," I say as she opens the passenger side door.

"I can't take Holly home with me tonight."

"But I can take her," Shelby jumps in. "Shawna would love to have a play date with Holly. We plan to make cookies tonight, and probably do a little decorating."

I look back and forth between the two women, not knowing what to say. I can't help but feel like this is a set-up, but I also can't leave work early to pick Holly up. I give in and nod. "Thanks, Shelby. I should be there shortly after five."

She waves me off. "No rush at all, Aiden."

"Meredith, can you tell Holly for me?" My sister nods and closes the door to my truck, so I can pull away. I tell myself that one time won't hurt anything and Holly would probably love spending time with Shawna. It's the other things that bother me: cookies and decorating. Both are two things I know Holly loves, but I can't provide for her right now.

When I get to the station, Eileen waves. "Fresh coffee in the back."

"Thanks. Hey, can you help me with something?"

"Anything, Fisher."

"I want to make cookies with Holly, but I'm not much of a baker."

"Say no more. There is ready-made dough at the grocers. I'll write the name down for you. It's straightforward and easy to use."

"Thanks, Eileen. Too bad you're with Dominic." Eileen knows I'm joking or maybe I'm not. I've known her since high school and can easily say, she's one of the good ones. Always has been. The rumor mill in town is saying Dom is going to ask her to marry him. If he doesn't, the line to start dating her will be long.

THREE

DELANEY

I startle awake. In a dazed confusion, I look around my living room for any sign of Trey. My television is on with the morning news. I'm confused.

"Trey?" I call out but don't receive a response. Gingerly, I stand and attempt to stretch the knots I have forming in my back from falling asleep while sitting up. My phone sits on the couch. I bend and tap the screen, but nothing happens. It must've died while I was waiting for Trey to arrive. Why didn't he wake me up? What time is it?

My muscles ache as I climb the stairs to the second floor. I make a mental note to add a couple of yoga sessions to my list of things to do while in Cancun. My bedroom door is closed, a sure sign Trey is in there, but why are we still sleeping? Surely, it's almost time for our car service to be here.

My heart pounds loudly, almost as if I'm on set and about to enter a room where I know I'm going to have to scream. I can't explain it, but this feeling doesn't sit well with me, neither does the fact that Trey didn't wake me when he got here last night.

Twisting the doorknob, I push the door open. The blackout curtains cloak the room in darkness. I flip on the light switch and stare at my still made bed. In fact, the only thing that seems amiss is Trey's bag seems to be gone.

Stupidly, I call out his name, but deep down I know he's not in my condo. Still, I look in my walk-in closet and walk into the bathroom, only to find both rooms empty. Frantically, I look around my room. The few things he kept on my dresser are gone, and the space he used in my closet is now empty. The tears come quickly, but they're irrational. There has to be some reasoning as to why his stuff is missing.

I rush back downstairs to grab my phone and plug it into the charger. I start to pace, waiting for the Apple symbol to appear and for my home screen to come alive. My phone vibrates with notifications. Mostly text messages from friends, but there are a few media alerts and emails. Opening the texting app, I scroll until I come to his name. And there it is.

Hey D. I didn't want to wake u, but I don't think things are going to work out between us. I hope you don't mind I took the tickets. I really need to get away & heal.

Heal?

He breaks up with me over text, steals my ticket to Cancun, and he needs to heal?

Right now, I'm squeezing the life out of my phone because I don't know what else to do. I don't want to cry, but I am because I don't understand what I did to deserve this. Why wouldn't he just talk to me and tell me he wasn't into the relationship? Why would he suggest we go away together?

My phone dings and I make the mistake of looking at it. It's an image of Trey at the airport with another woman. The headline is gut wrenching: **Hollywood starlet dumped for local waitress**... My next mistake is reading the beginning of the article.

It seems the relationship between Trey Baker and Delaney Du Luca is over. According to sources, Baker has been dating Kara Biondi for some time, and the two are expecting their first child this summer. Calls to Du Luca's rep went unanswered.

On cue, my phone rings and the text messages start to go crazy. I ignore them, needing some space to figure out what just happened to my life. How could I not see the signs? I'm so stupid. Relationships in Hollywood never last, and if I'm not the perfect example of that, I don't know who is.

I go back to Trey's text and reread it, hovering over his name. One press and my phone will call him. Will he answer? And if he does, what do I even say to him? I'm not sure I want to know what went wrong or why he's lied to me. It might be better for my self-esteem if I tell myself I didn't do anything wrong and Trey is nothing more than a jerk.

Instead of pulling on my big girl panties, I head to my room and collapse onto my bed to wallow in self-pity. I don't know if I'm heartbroken or humiliated. He could've easily just broken up with me. Why cheat? Why embarrass me?

The funny thing is, I can ask myself all of these questions, but I'll never get the answers. It's not like I'll ever call Trey or even speak to him when we're in the same social setting. I can even go as far to make sure he's never on the same set as me. As of now, I'm the bigger star and if I need to be a diva, I will.

I stay in bed, crying and screaming into my pillow until my head starts to hurt. When I get downstairs, the lack of decorations, especially for Christmas, bothers me. There's still three weeks until the big day, but I don't want to be alone.

Somewhere in the recesses of my couch, is my phone. I pull off the cushions, tossing them onto the floor until I find it. As if on cue, my mom's name lights up on my screen.

"Mom?" My voice sounds desperate, and maybe I am.

"Delaney, what am I reading?"

Sitting down on the hardwood of the sofa frame, I put my hand to my head. "I don't know. I had no idea something was wrong until I saw a text from him this morning, then the article. I'm completely blindsided."

"Are you okay?"

I shake my head knowing she can't see me. "Yeah, I guess. I don't know. I think I'm going to go buy a tree and decorate."

In the background, I hear her co-workers asking her what's going on. I swear Ramona Falls is worse than TMZ. "When do you start filming your next project?"

"Um..." I pause to think. "Mid-January or so."

"Come home, Delaney. It's been years, and we miss you. Everyone would be so excited to see you, and you can be here for the tree lighting ceremony. I would love to wake-up with you on Christmas morning and—"

As soon as my mom says the words 'Christmas' and 'home' I know deep in my mind that's where I need to be. "Mom, you don't need to convince me. I'll catch the next flight out. I think coming home will do me some good."

"She's coming home!" she yells to everyone at the bank. The cheers I hear bring a huge smile to my face. It's nice to feel wanted. "Do you want Dad to pick you up?"

"No, it's okay. I'll rent a car. I'll see you for dinner."

"I can't wait," she says before hanging up.

TRAVELING TODAY IS A MISTAKE. I should've known better than to fly out of a major airport, but they had the quickest flight to Vermont, and I didn't want to wait. With that said, I was completely unprepared for the onslaught of photographers shoving their cameras in my face as I walked into the airport. The last thing I wanted was to be reminded of what I read this morning, and to do so with a smile on my face.

Of course by the time I reach the terminal, the alerts are flooding my phone with images and posts about my dilemma. The vultures wasted no time broadcasting my apparent heartbreak with articles about me being despondent and hiding behind oversized sunglasses.

An airport security guard stands near me to keep people at bay. Typically, I wait in the lounge but didn't want to be bothered in there either. For now, I stand in the corner, watching planes coming in and out of the terminal, thinking back to a time when I used to do this when I was younger, and how life was simple.

Growing up in a small town where everyone knows everyone, people aren't like this. Or maybe they are, and I'm too naïve to think this type of drama happens in Ramona Falls. I can't imagine hearing about one of my friends being cheated on, not like this.

Before arriving at LAX, I sent a text to my friend

Mindy. She's the one person who has always been by my side and never asked for anything from me. To her, I'm just Delaney.

Mindy: **I'm so glad you're coming home.**

Me too.

Mindy: **We'll hang. Look for hotties. Hit the mall with disguises. Be girls.**

The idea of needing a disguise makes my stomach roll. I could go without one, put on a brave face and show everyone Trey Baker doesn't mean anything to me. Yeah, that's what I'm going to do because why not? Why should I hide when he's clearly not?

No disguise needed. Unless you don't want to be regulated to my picture taker?

Mindy: **I'll happily snap away for you.**

I'll text you as soon as I get home.

Mindy: **Can't wait. And don't let that man dampen your holidays. We're going to take your mind off of him.**

Thank you!

Going home is the right thing to do, even if it only means spending time with my family and Mindy. It'll be enjoyable to sit by the fire with my holiday leggings, big bulky sweaters, and oversized socks. That also means I'll have to hit the mall to do some serious shopping because I'm not prepared for the snow or the cold.

As soon as my flight is called, the security guard walks me to the gate. He wishes me a happy holiday before leaving me there, in line. A few people behind me murmur my name, and thankfully it's about my last movie, which did relatively well in theaters.

"Welcome, Ms. Du Luca," the ticket taker says as I hand her my boarding pass.

"Thank you." I'm the first one down the jetway, except for the people who need a bit more time to get to their seats. The flight attendant smiles as I step onto the plane. As soon as I sit down, she's offering me a drink. "Mimosa or screwdriver. I'm not picky," I request. I'm trying to be numb and get my vitamins in one fell swoop.

One of the nice things about a long flight is the ability to shut my phone off. And because the news about my current relationship status is fresh, I'm not being blasted all over any magazines. On a day that is possibly one of the worst of my life so far, it's the small things that are making me happy.

Unlucky for me, the woman sitting next to me is a fan. Generally, it doesn't bother me if someone makes contact or asks me a few questions, but the non-stop talking about everything I've done in my career is a bit much, especially when I'm not engaging. Right now, I'd love to continue drinking, but I told my mother that I'd rent a car. Otherwise, I'd be working on getting drunk right about now.

Yet, I continue to appease her, even when I have earplugs in and I'm trying to watch television. Each tap on my arm is met with a smile. Each question answered unless it's intrusive. Each joke laughed at. I ooh'd and ahh'd at her family photos and asked a few questions of my own.

And by the time the pilot comes over the loudspeaker to tell us we're landing, my flight has gone by quickly. When the plane pulls into our gate, we both stand and she holds her hand out.

"I read about what happened to you. I'm sorry, but that man doesn't deserve someone like you. I hope you find some happiness. I'm not normally like this, but you looked sad, and I wanted to cheer you up."

"Thank you," I tell her as we shake hands. "I really appreciate your company." I didn't know at first, but I'm thankful she kept my mind occupied elsewhere.

FOUR

AIDEN

*B*eing a police officer in Ramona Falls can be boring. I'm not complaining. I know the big city guys have it much harder, but I'd love to investigate something other than a missing bike, an overdue library book or someone skating on a frozen lake when they shouldn't be.

Right now, I'm parked inconspicuously on the outskirts of town, drinking warm coffee and listening to the chatter from the police scanner. Burlington is dealing with a drug bust, fire, and burglary, while I'm hiding in the bushes at the speed zone sign, waiting to catch someone with a lead foot.

I aspired to work for a bigger force, but when you have a family, you tend to make sacrifices, and when Heather... well, being a single parent really keeps you grounded. You're no longer making decisions for yourself, but also for your child and what they need. Their needs always come first.

My radar gun points at the oncoming traffic, calculating the speed of the people driving into town. Most of them are tourists, coming to check out our quaint little town and the massive amount of decorations our mayor insists we put up.

Honestly, though, I like them. They help me get into the spirit for the most part and they make Holly smile. Seeing Holly smile can really change my outlook sometimes.

I laugh when vehicles suddenly change their speed. It never fails. They ignore the change of speed warning and partially slow down after the speed has changed. Most of them do, except for this car coming toward me. Not only is the speed excessive, but also they're talking on their cell phone, which is against the law.

My adrenaline pounds as I flip the switch for my light bar, opting to keep my sirens off. I don't like to use them because it strikes curiosity in the neighbors, and more often than not, they'll come outside to be nosy. It's like getting a gold medal if you're the one to start the rumor mill in town. Unbelievably, women vie for this position, driving us men crazy.

Pulling out onto the two-lane highway, I press the accelerator, mostly because I can, to get behind the offending car. I radio in the license plate and hold my position until the driver pulls over.

Finally, the driver signals to pull over and I do the same, slanting my SUV a little to avoid being hit by oncoming traffic.

"It's registered to a rental agency. Hold, and I'll have a name for you."

"Thanks, Eileen. They've stopped, so I'm going to go have a chat."

"Roger that."

Every step I take toward the car is methodical. I'm checking for anything suspicious, listening for any odd sounds coming from the trunk or seeing if there's any recent damage done to the car, considering they were speeding away from something.

I tap on the window and lean down. The piercing green eyes of the woman in the driver's seat knock the wind right out of my sail. These are orbs I would know anywhere, yet I haven't seen them in ten plus years, not since our high school graduation. She smiles, and the simple act increases my adrenaline rush. For a moment, I feel like I'm a grasping for air.

"Fish, is that you?"

I take a step back, looking up and down the road, waiting for my colleagues to come out of the bushes to tell me they're playing some sort of practical joke on me because none of this makes sense. Why would Ramona Falls' biggest celebrity speed through town?

That's when it hits me, like a ton of concrete blocks. Not only have I pulled over the town sweetheart, but I'm going to be public enemy number one for doing so.

Placing my hands on her door, I lean in, trying not to stare at her out of fear I might fumble my words. "Laney?"

"Yeah. Don't you recognize me? I know it's been—"

"About ten years," I inject. I think every teenage boy in Ramona cried when she packed her bags and left for Hollywood. Each of us had aspirations of marrying her. Of course, I have the dubious title of saying I've dated her, even if it were only for a few months. Back then it felt like an eternity.

"Of course I do. I'm just a little taken back by seeing ya. What're doing here?"

"I'm home for Christmas," she says, holding her hands up as if it's no big deal. It's a huge deal. Massive, really. Once word spreads, people from all over will flock to our little town, hoping to catch a glimpse of her. Not to mention, the mayor will likely have us increase our police presence to protect her, which means overtime.

"Well, it's really good to see you. I bet your parents are happy to have you home." As soon as the words come out of my mouth, I realize I should've known she was coming back. It's not possible her mother kept this a secret. If you want to know anything about everything, Astrid Du Luca can tell you. "I'm surprised I hadn't heard you were coming back."

"Spur of the moment. The mill probably hasn't reached you yet."

I nod in agreement. "I'm gonna need your license and your rental information, Laney."

"What?"

I run my hand over my beanie, moving it back and forth until it's in a comfortable place. "You were speeding and talking on your cell phone. I gotta call it in."

Laney rolls her eyes before she starts rummaging through her bag. She's mumbling something, and from what I can gather by her hand flailing about, it's not pleasant. Her hand juts out the window with a small stack of documents. I take them and thank her as I head back to my patrol car.

As soon as I type her name into the Spillman database, her most current picture from The Department of Motor Vehicles pops up and I find myself once against staring, getting lost in her auburn hair and remembering the time I tried to count the freckles on her cheeks and nose. We may have dated for a few months, but have been friends our entire lives.

"Base to 8 2 4."

"Go ahead," I radio back.

"For all things holy, please tell me you did not pull over Delaney Du Luca," Eileen screeches into the radio.

"You pulled over my sister?" Dominic chimes in before I can even respond to Eileen.

"Fisher, I'm not sure I hear this correctly. Did you pull over the woman who put Ramona Falls on the map?" our chief asks next.

I rest my head against my steering wheel and count to ten. "Why did it have to be me?" I ask my empty car while my co-workers continue to squawk at me through the radio. When they finally grow silent, I reach for my handheld and press the button.

"She was speeding and talking on her phone."

Apparently, it doesn't matter, according to the chief. He's yelling into the radio, and anytime he takes a break, either Dom or Eileen start in on me. With my tail between my legs, I get out of the car and walk back to Laney. I tap on her window again and motion for her to roll it down.

"Here ya go, Laney."

"No ticket?"

I shake my head. She doesn't need to know I'd likely lose my job if I gave her one. Okay, that's may be a bit far-fetched, but I will suffer years of verbal attacks because no one forgets anything here. "Look, I know you haven't been home for a while, but we're handsfree here so just watch yourself when you leave town."

"Thanks, Fish. I really appreciate it."

With what redeeming quality I have left, I go back to my car. The standard procedure tells me I need to radio in and clear the scene, but I can't stomach the ridicule. It's bad enough I have to face my peers when I get back to the station.

As luck would have it, I follow behind Laney's car, and being the law-abiding citizen she is, she goes under the speed limit. I'm tempted to go by her, but Chief is big on us setting an example for the youth in the community. Still, when I signal to turn, I honk and wave at her, hoping she's not too upset with me.

Growing up in a small town, you're afforded certain liberties. Knowing the local police unit is one of them, even if they live in another town. For the most part, the members of the force have usually been our neighbors. For Dominic and Delaney, their father became mayor while we were in high school, and while Laney didn't do anything wrong, Dom tested the limits many times. I was right there along the side of him too, always trying to see how far we could go before someone busted us.

My cell phone rings. It sits on my dash so I can see who's calling. A picture of my mother flashes at me, and I press the green button and hit speaker so we can talk.

"Rough day?" she asks.

"Word spreads fast." I sigh.

"It's Ramona Falls."

"I know. Sadly, there isn't anything I can do about it. I was doing my job."

"I know. Do you want to come for lunch? Holly is about to go down and eat now."

The thought of spending some time with Holly brings a smile to my face. "I'll be right there." I hang up, and this time I do exceed the speed limit so I can get to the school in time.

My mom is waiting for me as soon as I pull up. She motions me to follow her in, even though I know where I'm going. A few kids say hi, and a couple of teachers scowl. Perfect. I'm going to go down in Falls history as the officer who pulled over Delaney Du Luca. Never mind the fact she was breaking the law.

The cafeteria is bustling with students. Mom and I get in line behind a class and wait for the staff to put our lunch onto a plate. It's some version of a turkey dinner, not that I mind. I actually enjoy the mashed potatoes.

"Holly's this way. She'll be excited to see you."

I'm glad my mom thinks so. Every day I sense a change in her. Holly was forced to mature to levels her friends aren't at yet. She's going to want more independence soon, and I'm not even close to the stage where I'm ready to let go. She's seven, not ten or fifteen. I still have time to be her daddy and not the man she's pissed at because she can't go out on a date. Yes, I will be the father who investigates who his daughter is dating.

"Hi, Grandma," Holly says as soon as my mom sits across from her. Holly's head turns slowly at my looming statue.

I smile and set my tray down.

"You can't sit here," she says so matter-of-factly that I pick the tray back up.

"Why not?" I ask as if I'm the new kid in school trying to sit at the popular table. I look from Holly to my mom, who shakes her head and closes her eyes briefly.

"Because you arrested Delaney Du Luca, Dad! Who does that? Are you trying to make it so I don't have any friends? Huh?" Holly throws her hands up in the air in the most overly dramatic fashion I have ever seen.

I look back at my mom for help. She doesn't offer any but does move over so I can sit next to her. I don't want to make a scene, but Holly needs to know she can't speak to me this way. After sitting down, I lean close to her, hoping she can hear me clearly, and that other eavesdropping ears aren't listening.

"It's my job to keep the streets of Ramona Falls safe, and if that means pulling someone over for breaking the law, I'm going to do it. It doesn't matter who it is. The law's the law, Holly."

Sitting back, I start to think I've done a fairly decent job until I see the look on Holly's face, followed by tears. "Daddy, she's my favorite, and you've ruined everything." She storms off, leaving her lunch untouched. My mom quickly follows, leaving me at a table with ten other seven-year-olds.

"Hey," I say, waving, but they're throwing daggers at me. "Right. I'll just eat my lunch then." This is likely the last meal I'll ever eat. I expect my lynching to happen by dinnertime, all because our town sweetheart had to break the law.

FIVE

DELANEY

*U*nder the potted plant, my parents still hide the key to their house. I slide it into the lock, turn and press down on the trigger to open the door. The smell of freshly baked cookies, cinnamon and the overall feeling of warmth washes over me. I close my eyes and inhale deeply, letting the stress of Hollywood leave me. It's good to be home.

I set my bags down in the entryway and take in the decorations. Garland and white lights wrap the staircase, with red bows scattered throughout. I'm eager to see our Christmas tree. When my parents had our family room remodeled, it became one of my favorites of the house, especially during the holidays. My mom always took decorating to a whole new level.

When I step into the kitchen, I'm surprised to find my mother... well, the backside of my mom because she's bent over with her head in the oven. I hadn't thought she'd be here, and the now fresh cookies I smelled when I walked in make sense. I wait until she pulls herself out before I alert her to my presence. She sits back on her heels, with black gunk all over her gloved hands.

"Hey, Mom."

"Delaney!" she screeches. She stands and walks toward me. I want to hug her, but the thought of getting dirty doesn't sit well with me. "Let me clean up. I wasn't expecting you for another hour or so."

"I thought I texted you my flight times." On the counter the cookies are calling my name. I grab one and bite into it. It's still warm, making the chocolate gooey. "So good," I mumble in between bites.

"You did, but I still get confused on the time zones. Now give me some sugar," she says once her hands are clean. I stuff the rest of the cookie into my mouth before falling into her arms. Unsuspectingly, tears start to fall as I bury my face in my mom's shoulder. I shouldn't cry over Trey, but I can't help the ache I feel in my heart. For a brief moment, I thought he was the one. I never thought he was having an affair or suspected him of being the type of man to do so. Now I wonder if I was his side-chick or a publicity stunt. I have a feeling it's the latter. It's a known fact in the industry that some people use others to advance their careers.

My mom continues to hold me, much like she's done time and time again, through the bumps and bruises, and other heartaches I've experienced over the years. I know it was only six months, but still. Knowing I didn't mean anything to him hurts.

I'm the first one to pull away. Mom runs her hands up and down my shoulders and offers me a soft smile. "You gonna be okay?" she asks.

I nod. "I am. I'm shocked and mad that I didn't know or

figure it out. Even thinking about him now, and his actions... I don't know. I didn't see him like this." I shrug and go back to the cookies. My mom hands me a plate, which I pile them on to. I go to the kitchen table and stare out the back window. "How come you don't have a tree yet?"

"Your dad has been busy and with neither you nor Dom living at home, it's hard to get into the spirit sometimes."

There's a deer traipsing through my parents' backyard, her hooves leaving indents in the snow. I watch as she heads to a bale of hay that my dad makes sure the animals have to eat during the winter.

"I've missed this," I say, motioning toward the yard. "Everything in Los Angeles is concrete. Sure, we have parks, but the houses and buildings are on top of each other. There's no space. No freedom."

"Are you talking about freedom from the press?" Mom asks from behind me. I turn to see her setting a glass of milk down onto the table. I smile and pull the chair out so I can sit down.

"Simplicity. The ability to breathe. I don't know. I can't explain it. As soon as I stepped outside, I felt a huge weight lifted off my shoulder. And yeah, the lack of paparazzi is a plus."

"Do they bother you much?"

I shrug and pick up another cookie, dunking it into my milk. "They do and don't. Obviously now, I'm a headline. The scorned girlfriend or the blind one who didn't know her boyfriend was cheating on her." I take another bite and chew.

"And now you're home, you're local news."

I look at her oddly. "What are you talking about?"

My mom smiles and starts laughing. "You were pulled over by Aiden Fisher for speeding."

"How do you even know that?"

She shrugs, as if it's no big deal. "Everyone knows."

I roll my eyes and shake my head. "Town gossip. I'm surprised you don't have a blog yet to keep everyone updated. You know you could probably do text alerts or something, save everyone time from playing telephone."

Mom laughs, but it's the truth. Astrid Du Luca is worse than the National Enquirer. "How was it seeing Aiden?"

"Fine. Why?"

"He's had a rough go of it lately."

"His wife has cancer, right?" I ask.

Mom shakes her head. "*Had* cancer, she died. Let's see, I think it's been a year and half now, maybe even two years. All I know is he's been struggling financially since Heather died. His insurance only covered so much of her medical expenses."

"That's so sad. They have a son, right?"

"Daughter. Holly, she's seven. He's such a good dad."

Aiden Fisher and I dated in high school. It was a few months, but my brother teased us so relentlessly that we decided to end it. They were friends and apparently, Dominic thought we were crossing some imaginary line. It was after I left for Hollywood, that he started dating Heather.

Mom's words weigh heavily on me. I can't imagine loving someone so much you devote your life to them, only to have them die, and at such a young age too. Maybe it's a good thing Trey did this to me before I was fully invested and ended up with a broken heart.

"What are you thinking about?"

I shake my head. "Nothing, really."

"I remember when you dated Aiden. Your dad and I thought for sure you would've married him."

My eyes meet hers, and she shrugs. "Why do you say that?"

"It was the way he looked at you, even before you both decided to start dating."

I try to think back to high school. I knew I wanted to move to Hollywood and act. It was my passion from the time I started in local theater. Everyone knew once I graduated, I was gone. My parents hated the idea. I promised them that if after one year I hadn't landed a major role, I'd come home. It took me six months, and I haven't looked back since. Picturing Fish when we dated is hard. It's been so long since I've thought about him. It's not like he's the one that got away or anything. We were friends because of my brother. We dated and ended it amicably, and stayed friends, although we didn't stay in touch with each other. The only one I really spoke to after leaving, aside from my family, is Mindy.

"I guess I don't remember."

"It was a long time ago."

It was, but it wasn't. Ten years isn't really that long ago. I should be able to recall how Aiden looked at me, but I guess I was lost in my own little world. "I think I'm going to go get settled."

I leave my mom in the kitchen and head back to the foyer to pick up my bags. It's been years since I've been in the cold weather and will need to go shopping. I'm hoping some of my old sweaters are still in my closet. Family photos cover the hallway walls. Climbing the steps, I stop at our most recent family photo, taken on the red carpet. My dad and Dominic are in tuxedos, while my mom and I are dressed in full-length gowns.

Stepping into my room is like walking through a time

warp. Nothing has changed. Including my twin sized bed or my dollhouse style bookshelves. The same bluish / greenish dresser with a mirror is there, in the same spot, I left it. It's funny I never upgraded my bed when I was in high school. I honestly think it was my father's way of keeping the boys out of my room.

I stand in my front of my bookcases, looking at everything I've collected over the years. They used to be my favorite things in my room and as I look around now, I think they still are. My room isn't large by any means, so my father tried to utilize the space best he could by giving me a place to, at first, store toys, which turned into trophies, photos and yearbooks.

Four books stand out the most to me. Maybe it's because Mom and I were just talking about high school or maybe I'm feeling a bit nostalgic because I'm home. I pull out the one for my senior year and open it. The page is full of short stories, random phone numbers and well wishes from my classmates. They all promised to go watch my first movie, making me wonder if they did.

My eyes land on Aiden's name. His handwriting was always so nice compared to other guys in our class.

Laney,

Our time was short, but sweet. I will miss your laugh, the way you tilt your head when you're thinking too hard, and the way you smile when you see me. Love, Fish

My fingers run over the page, feeling the indent from his words. I've never wondered what it would've been like if I stayed in Ramona Falls or if I had gone away to college, and come home during breaks and summer vacations. What if Dom hadn't been so crass about the relationship between Fish and I, would we have dated longer? Many of my classmates married their high school sweethearts. Some stayed here and started raising families, while others moved. What would my life be like if I hadn't followed my dream of becoming an actress?

Closing the book, I set it down on my bed and head to the cabinet, which is part of my dresser. I pull the door open and drop to my knees. My mom must've taken the liberty of preserving my favorite sweaters because they're all in there, sealed tightly in those plastic vacuum bags you see late night infomercials for.

I stay up in my room, unpacking. Every so often, my mom comes up to chat, telling me about the latest gossip. That's the thing about Ramona Falls, gossip changes here like a clock changes time. Nothing gets past my mother, which is probably another reasons why I never dated seriously in high school. I can't even imagine how I'd feel if someone told my mom they caught me making out behind the shed at the lake. It'd be so embarrassing. It's ironic that I moved away from here to Hollywood, which is an even bigger place for juicy details. It seems I need the gossip to survive.

When I was little, I used to wait for my dad to come home from work by sitting on my knees on my mother's "do not touch" couch with my stomach pressed to the back, trying to get as close to the window as possible. I'd wait until his car pulled into the driveway, then I'd rush to the door, eager to give him a hug. I remember he smelled like oil from working at the factory. I used to love that smell.

It wasn't until I was in high school when he ran for mayor and won. Honestly, no one expected him to win because he lacked experience, but the margin of victory was a landslide and we went from a blue-collar family to what I call a dingy-white collar family. My mom still works at the bank. My brother's a police officer. While I may be an actress, I've never forgotten my roots.

And that is why I'm sitting on my mother's sofa, with my chin resting on my hands, watching and waiting for the headlights of my dad's car to appear so I can run to the door and wrap my arms around his shoulders.

SIX

AIDEN

I wish I could say my day became increasingly better after my attempted lunch with Holly, but it didn't. Eileen and Dominic took it upon themselves, probably with great pleasure, to decorate my locker with pictures of Delaney and left comments all over them, making it seem as if Delaney were asking for leniency with her speeding ticket. She didn't receive a ticket, so their joke is not very funny. Although, when I saw my locker, I looked past the ridiculous words and focused on her beauty. She was a stunner back in high school, and now she's even more gorgeous. Now that I've seen her in the flesh, I can't shake her from my mind.

As for the rest of my day, I'm currently parked outside of Shelby's house, contemplating what I'm going to say to her when I knock on the door to retrieve Holly. I rehearse the words repeatedly, thanking her for taking her after-school. In my mind, I reach for Holly's hand and we beat feet to the truck before Shelby can say anything.

Every so often, I look toward her house and see her standing in her large picture window. I hope that she knows it's me, lurking in the darkness, and isn't about to call the police on me, not least because if she did, it'd likely be one of my colleagues who answered the call and I've had enough teasing from them today. It's hard though, to get out of the truck and walk toward the door. I don't know if it's because when I look at her house, I envision what Heather and I had thought our living room would look like at Christmas time, with a large tree lit and decorated for our neighbors to see. Knowing that reality is so far from happening really twists the knife in my chest, yet I'm determined to make it happen for Holly.

Shelby opens the door before I have a chance to ring the doorbell. Instantly, I'm swaddled in warmth. "Come in," she says, holding the screen door open. I do, and stand on the doormat, waiting for Holly to come rushing at me. Shelby brushes against me as she closes the door. I want to think it's innocent, but I'm not so sure. My sister has been trying to push us together for months now. "You can come in. The girls are in the kitchen." Shelby motions toward her kitchen, at least I'm assuming it's where her kitchen is located.

"Do I need to take off my shoes?"

"Nah, don't worry about them." She motions again, and this time I follow her into her large kitchen where her daughter, Shawna, and Holly are setting the table.

"Hey, Daddy, you're just in time for dinner."

"Dinner?" I ask, looking from my daughter to Shelby and back again.

"The girls were hungry and I didn't want to spoil their dinner with cookies so I made a batch of spaghetti. You're welcomed to stay."

By the looks of the table, they were expecting me to stay. I don't want to be rude, but I also want to get home. Holly and I need to have a long talk about manners and respect, especially when we're in public. However, by the look I'm getting from my daughter, leaving now isn't an option. Yet another point I'm going to have to talk to her about.

"Thanks." I nod at Shelby, who returns my gesture with a smile. "So where am I sitting?" I ask the girls as I make my way to the table. There are four places set, two on each side. Both girls point, opposite of where they're standing. I have a feeling this is a set-up though, especially as they both sit across from me.

Shelby brings everything to the table and refuses to let me help her. I feel like a clod, sitting here, as if she's supposed to serve me. I should be doing something since she slaved over the stove to prepare a meal for my daughter and me, and even though it's only pasta, there's still an effort needed.

After Shelby places the food on the table, I stand and dish up the plates for the girls. It's the least I can do. Much to Holly's displeasure, I make her a bowl of salad, knowing it's not her favorite. She eyes me, but doesn't say anything, which is probably for the best.

"How was work?" Shelby asks after she sits down. I pause, mid-bite and let her question sink in. I don't know her, at least not well. We see each other at school, our girls play together, and my sister talks about her non-stop, but that's the extent of our relationship. I suppose, sitting at her table and eating her food has moved us to a different status.

"He pulled over Delaney Du Luca," Holly says for me, shaking her head. I do believe there's a slight eye roll going on as well.

"I heard that, but it took me awhile to piece together why everyone was up in arms."

I clear my throat after swallowing. "Laney's from here,"

I tell Shelby. "She's Ramona Falls' sweetheart. Plus, her dad is the mayor."

Shelby nods and returns her attention to her food. I do the same and try to keep my head down.

"But other than embarrassing the actress, work went well?"

"Yeah, I mean there isn't much happening in Ramona Falls."

"I once had my dolly stolen from my front yard. My mama called you, but you never came," Shawna says as she sits back in her chair and crosses her arms.

I glance at Shelby, who looks mortified. I have a feeling she never called, but told Shawna she did. "I'm sure if I were working that day, I would've come right over and investigated."

Shelby's leg touches mine under the table. I'm going to take that as her silent thank you and let it go so I can enjoy the dinner she's prepared for us. Throughout the course of the meal and dessert, the girls tell us about their day, talking about art class and how they're having to create their own snowmen for the winter festival coming up. They tell us their artwork will be on display for everyone to see.

"We should take the girls," Shelby suggests. I find myself tongue-tied at the suggestion, so I do the only conceivable thing I can think of, and nod.

After dinner, I help clear the table while Holly gets her stuff together. "Thank you for dinner, Shelby. You really didn't have to do this." I set the plates down in the sink full of water and turn to face her. Her hand rests on my bicep as she looks into my eyes.

"I wanted to, Aiden. The girls get along so well, and I just hate to think of you and Holly alone all the time."

We're not alone if we're together, right? Although, there

are times when I feel utterly shut off from life because of my situation. "Thanks, but we're good. We make it work." Shelby steps closer, closing the gap between us. I know if I step back that'll drive the message home that I'm not interested. But maybe I am. Maybe it's time for me to move on and start a relationship with someone. Shelby's a good person. She's involved with the Parent-Teacher Association, is Holly's Girl Scout leader, and volunteers at the school when needed. She moved here about a year ago, wanting a quiet life after her divorce. "I should probably get Holly home and in bed," I tell her. She smiles softly and follows me to the door.

"You know, Holly is welcome here whenever. I don't mind."

"Thanks, Shelby." I nod and clear my throat to get Holly's attention. "Are you ready?"

Holly begrudgingly drags herself to the door, stopping every few seconds to give Shawna a hug goodbye. Don't they realize they'll see each other tomorrow? As soon as the thought rushes through my head, I know tomorrows are never guaranteed. Holly and I know that better than anyone does.

"Bye, Aiden," Shelby says after I step by her. Short of thanking her again, for dinner, I feel like I'm supposed to say or do something. Is a kiss on the cheek required here? I don't want to send her the wrong message, but I want her to know I'm appreciative of the effort she's put in. I muster up a smile and wave, and head to my truck with Holly dragging behind me.

"Hop in." I give Holly a little boost into the cab of the truck and make sure she's buckled into her booster seat before I shut the door.

"Did you have fun? I forgot to make sure you picked up the toys you played with."

"I did," she tells me, although I'm not sure which she's referring to. Holly looks out the window, focused on the houses that have been decorated extensively as we drive home. "Can we put lights up?"

"Sure." I make a mental note to ask my dad for a box of outside lights. It's an expense I can't justify right now. *But if you had a partner, expenses would be split.* I don't know where that thought has come from, but I'm not sure I like it. Or maybe I do and it's my subconscious telling me I need to find someone suitable for Holly and I. Young girls need a mother. "I want to talk to you about your outburst at school today."

"I was angry."

"I get that, Holly, but it was inappropriate and rude. You're seven and you don't have the right to speak to me like that, especially in front of others. If you're angry with me over something, we can sit down and discuss it. However, when it comes to my job, you don't have a voice in how I do my work. It doesn't matter if I pulled over Delaney Du Luca or the President of the United States. The fact is, she was speeding, which means she's breaking the law."

"It's embarrassing. All the kids were laughing at me."

"Well, imagine how Delaney felt when she was pulled over for breaking the law. Don't you think she was embarrassed?"

"I guess." She sighs.

As soon as we pull into the garage, Holly hops out of the truck. She's kind enough to turn the light on for me so I'm not blindly walking around while I close up. "I'll start your bath as soon as I get inside."

45

"Okay. Can we get a cat?" she asks from the doorway. I turn and look at her, puzzled by her question.

"Um... no."

"Why not?"

Because I can barely afford to feed us, let alone a pet. "I'm not a fan of cats, Holly."

"How about a puppy?"

I close the garage door and flip off the light, motioning for her to go inside. "No pets, at least not right now. Maybe over the summer we can talk about it." Inside, the house is cold. Nothing screams I need to make a change like walking into a house and still seeing your breath.

"It's cold," Holly says as she uses her hands to warm up her arms.

"I'll turn on the heat. Go start your bath, I'll be there in a minute." I watch as Holly makes her way to the bathroom. She closes the door and the sound of the pipes coming to life tells me she's turned on the water. I stand there, in the dark, listening to the furnace come on and the baseboards creak. My hands clench as tears threaten to make an appearance. I don't know what I'm supposed to do, but I feel like I can't provide for my daughter. It's this house, the medical bills, and the fact that I don't make enough to cover everything.

Someday. That's my mantra. Someday everything is going to work out. Someday the bills will be gone and I'll be able to do what I need to do to fix this house and give Holly the home Heather and I wanted to give her.

SEVEN

DELANEY

I never thought I'd have to step foot again in what used to be my favorite mall. Yet, here I am among the feisty shoppers, fighting for the last prized Christmas toy, when all I want is a nice pair of boots, some thick socks, maybe a coat and a few scarves, and if I'm lucky, a pair of ice skates because the ones left over from my adolescent years have seen better days. All things I need in order to survive the harsh winter weather of Vermont.

I'm shoulder bumped, cut in front of and side swiped as I make my way toward one of my beloved stores. I have every intention of getting what I need and getting the hell out of Dodge. I'm no match for these mothers and their battle for holiday shopping greatness.

It's been a few days since I arrived back in town. I was foolish to think everyone would drop what they're doing to entertain me, forgetting people have lives here. Jobs, families, bills to pay, all while I'm on vacation and already bored out of my mind. I know I should use the time to relax, maybe catch up on some reading, and learn to just be me again without having my name attached to a project or whomever I'm dating. I should find myself and go back to my roots, and that's what I'm going to do.

With my hair tucked under my beanie, I meander in and out of stores. Even though I have a list, I've already veered off and bought a few things at Guess, Burberry, Anthropologie, and Calvin Klein, realizing I need Christmas presents for everyone.

For the past two stores though, I feel like someone has been following me. Normally, said person would have a camera stuck to their face, but not here, and each time I look over my shoulder, they turn away. I'm not naïve enough to think I won't be noticed, but the thought did cross my mind that I'd be able to get my shopping done without anyone recognizing me.

Apparently, that's not the case as the person has followed me out of the store. My steps become a bit faster and my head feels as if it's on a swivel as I try to find a security guard, but the only people I spot are a group of women, both young and old, with their cell phones out and poised for action. Turning around, I realize I'm trapped and have unfortunately found myself cornered in by nothing but walls. I can't even escape into a store to ask for help.

The women surround me, saying my name and asking me to look their way. They've seen one too many Entertainment Weekly red carpet broadcasts in my opinion. I frantically look everywhere but at them, hoping they comprehend that they're scaring me, and this isn't the way to get me, let alone anyone, to do as they demand.

Questions are tossed at me, asking me why Trey and I broke up, did I know about the baby, am I jealous, am I pregnant, and what am I doing here. Some tell me they're my biggest fans while trying to get me to pose for a selfie. If the onslaught wasn't so pushy, I may oblige them, but my fight or flight is kicking in and everything within is telling me to run.

They're closing in, making their semi-circle around me even smaller and pushing me into the wall as much as possible. I don't think I'd be able to escape, even if I tried. The mob mentality right now is ridiculous, and the people walking by have joined in.

"Please, if you'll back up, I'll answer questions." My plea falls on deaf ears. The questions come faster and are more personal. Clearly, whatever they read about me in the tabloids isn't enough and they want more.

"Hey, what's going on here?" a voice breaks through the crowd. It's loud and forceful. Finally, security has seen the gang of shoppers crowding me. "Back up. There's nothing to see here. Get moving." The phrases this man uses as he pushes through the crowd slightly put me at ease. It isn't until I look up that I see the well-known face of Fish, pulling people out of his way and shoving through others who won't budge.

When his eyes land on mine, the familiar gaze he's always given me provides me with a bit of hope in this situation. "Laney," he says my name almost as if he hasn't seen me in years, rather than days. I nod. It's an automatic response. He turns and holds something in his hand above the crowd. I believe it's his badge, but I'm not certain. Does he have any authority here? "All right folks, get moving." He holds his other arm out in an effort to protect me while I cower behind him.

From what I can tell, pictures are still snapped or at least a video or two is being made. I have no doubt I'll be all over social media in a matter of seconds, which will send my public relations team into a frantic mode of 'what the hell is she doing without Calvin?'. It's my fault for thinking I could duck in and out without being detected. Lesson learned, the hard way.

"Thank you, Fish," I say, as my arms wrap around his waist and my head rests on his back. I don't know what has spurred me to show this type of affection. Maybe it's because I'm grateful he's saved my life.

He taps my hand. I take this as a sign he'd like me to remove the vise-like grip I have on him right now. I do and he turns around. His smile is soft, but his eyes tell a different story. They're cold, and scary and similar to the way Dominic looks when he's angry. I chalk this up to Aiden being a police officer. I caress the rough stubble of his cheek with the back of my fingers, watching as his blue eyes soften from my touch.

"Thank you, Aiden." I can't remember the last time I've used his name. In fact, I can't recall a time when I ever have. He's always been Fish to me and I was his Laney. He's the only one I ever allowed to call me by a shortened version of my name.

"I'm glad I was here to help."

I take a small step back and look at his attire. He's in jeans, a flannel shirt and his snow boots are unlaced, giving off a sex appeal that I haven't seen in a long time. "What are you doing here? Shouldn't you be working?"

Fish runs his hand over his short hair. He looks left, then right before focusing his attention on me. "I'm supposed to be shopping for Holly, but as you can see I haven't been doing very well." He holds up his empty hands.

I think back to the other day when my mother was filling me in on Aiden's life. Holly is his daughter. I believe she's seven. I don't remember what I liked when I was seven, and can't imagine how hard it is for him to shop for her. But I do know what's popular among girls now. "Tell you what. Since you helped me, I'll help you shop."

His eyes go wide and he nods rapidly.

"But... first we have lunch because I'm starving." I link my arm inside of his and pull him along, only to disengage out of fear. Not for me, but for Aiden. The last thing he probably wants is to have his face splattered all over the rag mags being labeled as my next boyfriend. Honestly, having the press invade my life while I'm home would be very upsetting. If this mall excursion isn't enough to keep me indoors until I leave, I don't know what else is.

Aiden and I stop at one of the many restaurants in the mall. The hostess recognizes me immediately and fumbles over her words as she tries to find out how many people are in our party.

"Only two, and someplace with a bit of privacy and away from the windows, please." I know it's an oxymoron to ask for privacy in a mall, but I'm hoping the message is sent loud and clear – we don't want to be bothered. I motion Aiden to lead while I follow closely behind with my head down. As long as I watch his feet, I shouldn't stumble. I'm tempted to reach out and hold onto the back of his shirt or even his belt loop, but don't want to send the wrong message.

"Will this work, Miss Du Luca?"

I look up and nod. "Yes, thank you." The hostess hands us our menus after we've taken our seats. I peruse it briefly, figuring out that a salad is really the only option for me and close it. I use this time to study Aiden, and the fine lines he's developed in the last ten years. His brows furrow as he reads over the menu and his forehead is wrinkled. He focuses hard, his lips purse and he lets out random sighs until he closes it. "Did you find something?"

"Yes, I'm going to get the chip appetizer," he says without making eye contact. I grab the menu and flip it open. Not because I want the same thing, but because I want to see the price. Maybe I'm over thinking, but why would anyone eat chips for lunch, unless he's already eaten.

"Have you had lunch?"

He shakes his head no.

"So why the chips?"

Aiden's head tilts to the side briefly before shaking his head again. "I just—"

"It's on me, okay? You rescued me and this is the way I can repay you, so you order what you want and be prepared for me to pick off your plate."

He smiles and leans forward. His hands are under the table and I can feel his fingers brushing against my knees. They're just as ticklish now as they were in high school. I wonder if he remembers this.

"Let me get this straight. Little Miss Hollywood still picks food off others' plates?"

I lean forward, so we're closer. "First, don't call me that ridiculous nickname. Second, only the plates of people I like. Third, you know I'll order a salad and hate it so you best order a monster cheeseburger with bacon and fries so I have something to eat. I may have been gone for ten years, but I haven't changed."

"That much," he adds.

My mouth drops opens, and I lean back until I'm resting against the booth. "What do you mean?"

Aiden shrugs. "I see the magazines every now and again, listen to what Dom says."

Shaking my head, I narrow my eyes at him. "I haven't changed, except for the fact that living in the land of sun is the most amazing feeling ever. Although, I never thought I missed the snow until I was standing in the dining room the other day and saw a deer cross my parents' backyard. I don't know, there's something about fresh snow..."

"It's magical."

I smile. "Yeah, it is." Before I can say anything else, our waiter appears. He asks for our drink order, which we give, but also tell him we're ready to order. Of course, I stick with my Cobb salad and Aiden orders the bacon double cheese-burger with fries and onion rings. As soon as he adds the onion rings, my lips purse. I like his style. Once the waiter leaves, I lean forward again. "So tell me what your daughter likes."

"You," he says.

"Excuse me?"

Aiden laughs and fiddles with his napkin. "My daughter is obsessed with you. She yelled at me after she heard I pulled you over. It's as if I ruined her life. Funny thing is, I had no idea she even knew who you were until the other day, but she hasn't stopped talking about you since."

"Well, I'll have to make sure you look like a hero to her then, won't I?"

His eyes pierce mine, making me want to ask him what his story is. I *know* him, but people change. What makes Aiden Fisher tick these days? I'm here until after the New Year, I might as well spend it with my friends from high school. It just so happens that Aiden is one of those.

EIGHT

AIDEN

*E*ach morning I wake up, determined to make today a better day than yesterday. It's not that all my days are bad, but the holidays seem to increase my stress level. It's hard, when every day I worry about my financial situation, but add the pressure of being Santa, and the strain goes through the roof, especially when I know that what little savings I have could be used elsewhere.

As much as I'd like to tell Holly about Santa, I can't. She's already lost so much in her young life, destroying what little magic she believes in would devastate her. But being at the mall, and seeing all these other people with their arms full of bags really does something to one's psyche. Nothing like driving home the stake in the middle of my chest, pointing out that I can't afford the best new toys on the market.

Each store I step into, my blood pressure rises. Even the sale prices seem to be over the top, but I'm not left with many choices. Santa has to have something under the tree for Holly, and it can't be coal because that's what he's leaving for me.

I'm overwhelmed by the sheer amount of "must haves" and "every kid's dream" displays. They're enough to drive me out of the store and back into the masses of holiday shoppers. I stop and look into the windows of each store, hoping that something will jump out and scream at me, telling me Holly *needs* whatever it may be. But nothing does.

What does catch my attention is the group of people who all have their cell phones raised in the air. That right there is enough to heighten my senses that something is going on that shouldn't be. I look around for security, shocked to find no one. I can't, in good conscience, walk away.

A group of onlookers is one thing, but when you have a cluster of people together, speaking loudly with their cell phones out, it usually signals trouble. "Hey, what's going on here?" I ask as I push my way through the crowd while telling them to step away. These people though, they're persistent and push back, determined to get to whatever or whoever they're surrounding. "Back up. There's nothing to see here. Get moving."

Except, there's everything to see. Laney is cowering in the corner, pressed against the wall with nothing but fear in her eyes. My instinct is to pull her into my arms, to shelter her from these women, but she's used to this, right? Maybe not this aggressively, but surely she's accustomed to people acting in this fashion.

"Laney," I say her name softly. I don't know if it's because I'm shocked to find her like this or because she's simply one of the most beautiful women I've ever known. It took me a long time after she left to realize what I let slip through my fingers. Her brother was and still is my best friend, and I don't think he took too kindly to us dating.

Dominic never came out and said as much, but the side comments were there.

She broke up with me. Even though we had only dated for a few months, I was heartbroken. It wasn't long after Laney moved to Los Angeles that I met Heather. Our first date was one of Laney's movies. That's when it hit me. I would never be her leading man.

Without turning around, I hold my badge up while my eyes are trained on Delaney's. "All right folks, get moving." I finally turn around and use my free arm to shield her, and when she uses my back to hide, wrapping her arms around my waist, I feel this crazy surge of energy.

Once everyone has dissipated, I tap her hand to let her know it's safe to come out from behind me. When I turn around I see a look of panic in her eyes and I hate it. I hate that someone put her in this situation, despite her profession. My hands clench at my sides as my temper starts to flare. I want to shake those people, demand they give her an apology, but it would likely fall on deaf ears.

She thanks me, and I swallow hard at the way my name falls from her lips. My memory bank fails me. I can't recall a time when she's ever said "Aiden", always choosing to use the nickname she gave me so many years ago. Laney's hand brushes along my cheek. Her touch is soft against my rough stubble. I'm tempted to grasp her wrist so I can hold her hand there, but I don't want to scare her. I haven't been touched like this in years, not since Heather, and I'm not sure how I should feel or if I'm thinking too much of the gesture. It's simple, loving, and shouldn't mean anything to me.

"I'm glad I was here to help." My words feel jumbled and incoherent, but she smiles so I must've made some sort of sense. She steps back and isn't shy about the way she's looking at me. I feel the heat rise to my cheeks as I stand there under her microscope. "What are you doing here? Shouldn't you be working?" she asks.

"I'm supposed to be shopping for Holly, but as you can see, I haven't been doing very well."

Delaney smiles. But it's different from others. It seems mischievous and I have a feeling I'm about to regret being in this mall.

"Tell you what. Since you helped me, I'll help you shop."

I hate shopping, and I'd be a fool to pass this up. I nod frantically, feeling like a dog begging for a treat.

"But... first we have lunch because I'm starving." She doesn't wait for my response before linking arms with me. We only get a few steps away before she removes her arm. I get it. I'm not the type of guy she's usually attached to and probably doesn't want to have to explain what she was doing with a country bumpkin. I try not to let any of this bother me. She's a big time Hollywood actress. I'm nobody, but a guy she dated a long time ago.

As soon as we enter one of the staple restaurants at the mall, the hostess's eyes all but bug out of their sockets. *Believe me, I feel the same way.* I smile and pretend this is an everyday occurrence for me, hanging out with Delaney Du Luca.

"Only two, and someplace with a bit of privacy and away from the windows, please," Laney tells the star-struck hostess.

"Will this work, Miss Du Luca?"

"Yes, thank you."

I sit across from her, but for a moment I think about sitting on the same side to offer her a bit of shelter from the other patrons, but as I look around, it'll be no use. People are already recognizing her.

The prices on the menu make my stomach flip. Anything extra goes right to the pile of medical bills. Eating out is a frivolous expense I rarely partake in. I settle on the cheapest item and close the menu.

"Did you find something?"

"Yes, I'm going to get the chip appetizer."

Laney opens her menu back up and looks until she lands on my selection. There's a noticeable tick in her jaw, which means she's about to unleash one of her famous tantrums. Back in high school, we all knew when she was about to explode. Her jaw tightens, her eyes wander and her lips do this thing that can only be described as pursing and smashing together. I know I'm in for it now.

"Have you had lunch?" she asks, almost as if I'm ten years old.

I shake my head.

"So why the chips?"

"I just—"

"It's on me, okay. You rescued me and this is the way I can repay you, so you order what you want and be prepared for me to pick off your plate."

I smile and lean forward. My hands are under the table and I don't know what possesses me to do this, but my fingers brush against her knees. Laney doesn't move, so I continue to do it, wondering if she's still ticklish there. "Let me get this straight. Little Miss Hollywood still picks food off others' plates?"

She closes the distance between us. "First, don't call me that ridiculous nickname. Second, only the plates of people I like. Third, you know I'll order a salad and hate it so you best order a monster cheeseburger with bacon and fries so I have something to eat. I may have been gone for ten years, but I haven't changed." Her rant is adorable, if not a little child-like. Yet, I like it. She's like a breath of fresh air that I desperately need.

"That much."

Her mouth drops open, and she leans back against the booth. "What do you mean?"

I shrug, wishing I could get up and go sit next to her, but I can't. "I see the magazines every now and again, listen to what Dom says."

"I haven't changed, except for the fact that living in the land of sun is the most amazing feeling ever. Although, I never thought I missed the snow until I was standing in the dining room the other day and saw a deer cross my parents' backyard. I don't know, there's something about fresh snow..."

"It's magical."

"Yeah, it is." She doesn't say anything else as our waiter appears. I appease her by ordering what she wants, but add onion rings as well. Deep down, Laney is a food junkie and I imagine having to look a certain way in front of the cameras might take its toll. If I can make her smile, I'm going to do it.

"So tell me what your daughter likes."

"You," I tell her unabashedly.

"Excuse me?"

I chuckle and take one of my hands out from underneath the table so I can fidget with the napkin. My other though, it's still under the table, my fingers still brushing against her knee every chance I get. "My daughter is obsessed with you. She yelled at me after she heard I pulled you over. It's as if I ruined her life. Funny thing is, I had no idea she even knew who you were until the other day, but she hasn't stopped talking about you since."

"Well, I'll have to make sure you look like a hero to her then, won't I?"

I'm at a loss for words, which seems to be okay since our food has arrived. Honestly, I'm thankful for the quick service. Eating gives my mouth something to do other than try to say things I shouldn't, like telling her she's beautiful, that everyone in Ramona Falls loves her, that my wife was a big fan and used to ask me questions as her death neared, and whether I ever thought about Delaney. Truth is, I hadn't. She was so far from my mind and just a part of my history.

No sooner than the waiter puts our plates down, is her hand reaching across the table. I laugh, relishing in the fact that some things never change. It feels good to be out like this, with her. To be able to let go some of the stress I'm feeling and possibly enjoy shopping, knowing she's going to be by my side later.

"This is so good," she says as she takes a bite of the onion ring. "Like, I haven't had one of these in years."

"Why not?"

"Because everyone is always watching. They're waiting for people like me to screw up so they can capitalize on it."

I pick up my burger and take a few bites. Random pieces of bacon fall onto my plate and before I can grab them, she snatches them up. "What's the worst thing they've said about you that was true?"

Laney stabs her salad with her fork as if it's offended her somehow. "That I can't keep a man," she says, sighing.

I'm not sure what the right response is, but I reach across the table and rest my hand on hers. "Somehow I don't think that's true." I know it isn't because she could've easily kept me.

Laney's eyes shoot up and connect with mine. I smile, but she doesn't. I start to remove my hand from her, realizing I've overstepped my boundaries, only to find her fingers interlocking with mine.

As soon as our waiter steps to our table, she pulls her hand back. I try not to let the sudden movement mean anything. I get it. She has appearances to keep up, and I don't fit the mold, which when I think about it, is fine. Laney and I are in two very different places in our lives, and will likely never be on the same page.

NINE

DELANEY

"So besides me, what else does Holly like?" I ask as Fish and I walk through the aisle of a department store. When we first walked in, I went right for the toddler section and started piling things into my arms. It wasn't until he asked who I was shopping for did it hit me that I have absolutely no clue what size a seven year old is. He was gracious enough to steer me in the right direction, but I quickly found the clothes aren't the same. They're not as soft and fun. These designers are trying to make these little girls look like teens.

"Wonder Woman, Barbies," he says as he checks the tag of the outfit I'm holding up. He grimaces and shakes his head. "She likes to draw, color. I don't know, I guess she's your average second grader."

"When I was in second grade I had my dad build me a stage in the garage so I could perform for the neighborhood." I shrug. I thought I was normal until my elementary classmates started making fun of me. Dolls only interested me if they were part of my productions.

Aiden laughs. "Do you ever think about directing?"

I shake my head. "I love what I do, but being behind a camera really isn't my thing."

"But you thought about it in high school. I remember you mentioned it one time in passing, something about how the drama teacher wasn't listening to your direction."

"Plays are different," I tell him.

He leans against the rack, bringing himself closer to me. "What about while you're here then? The kids will do their holiday play for the festival. You could direct that."

I look at Aiden as if he has two heads. He must be crazy thinking I could direct a bunch of kids in a production when I can barely keep my life on track. I put the outfit that I've been holding back on the rack and step away. I don't know why it's bothering me so much that Aiden suggested this. Maybe because deep down, I'd love to direct a play or two in my spare time, even act on Broadway under the bright lights with a live audience where I can see judgment on their faces. Call me crazy, but seeing whether or not I move people or evoke some sort of emotion would be a high-light of my career.

Aiden reaches for my hand, halting my fleeing feet. "Did I say something wrong?"

"Not at all." *No, you said everything right*, but I'm so lost in my own head to actually make something like this work. But in the few short seconds I thought about it, I've realized it's something I want to do.

"Are you sure because back there..." he turns and looks over his shoulder. Surprisingly, I do too, hoping to find a shadow of myself, pointing and mocking me for being so indecisive and closed-minded.

I take a deep breath and look around. A few people are staring, but thankfully, they don't have their phones out. "Is the festival still three days?"

Aiden smiles brightly, almost as if he knows he's won some great prize. "No, it's four. Two full weekends now. The first weekend is the tree lighting ceremony on Friday night. Saturday is all day with vendors, and there's an igloo and snowman competition, plus the play and the dance, and Sunday is the hockey game. Your dad changed it about three years ago to give people more time."

"Dance?" I question.

"A few years back the council came up with a dance party. Adults only." Aiden stuffs his hands into his pockets.

"They did? Huh, my parents never mentioned it. I bet they like to dance all night."

"Right along with my parents."

"Do you still skate in the hockey game?" At the conclusion of every winter festival, everyone gathers at the lake for a round-robin tournament. Most of the time, the games last well into the wee hours of the next morning. Dominic and Aiden had been on the same team the last I knew.

Aiden steps toward me, bridging the gap between us. The smell of his cologne is subtle, yet familiar. "I do. It's really the one time I can hit someone and not get into trouble because I'm a police officer."

I laugh and shake my head, the motion bringing us even closer. "Dom says the same thing." When I look up at Aiden, he's smiling.

"Ahem, excuse me, but may I have a photo with you?"

Instantly, I step away from Aiden and focus on the young girl standing at my side. I nod and wait for her to stand next to me, expecting her to take a selfie, but she doesn't. Instead she hands her phone to Aiden, without even asking him if he'd mind taking a picture. I'm embarrassed and can feel frustration boiling within. It's rude to assume someone is going to take your picture, especially if they haven't offered or been asked. I try to make eye contact with Aiden, but he's not looking at anything but the phone in his hand. He steps in front of us, and I stand as still as I can, while he snaps the picture. I'm not sure I even smile.

"Here ya go," Aiden says as he hands the phone back to the girl. Only now, a line has now formed, and Aiden is struggling with the amount of phones he has in his hands. After the tenth photo, I sigh heavily, wishing my assistant or Calvin were with me so I could be done already.

"Delaney, are you ready?" My heart sinks a bit when he uses my name, but I know it's because others are around. I nod and reach for his extended hand, linking my fingers through his. A small giggle escapes as he makes a mad dash for the entrance. The small crowd we left behind yells out my name, but he continues to keep a brisk pace, weaving us in and out of the shoppers.

We duck into the Disney store and I immediately let out a squeal of delight. I love this store, and everything it represents. "We'll definitely find presents here," I tell him. Aiden glances at me, and then his eyes fall to our joined hands. I should let go, but I don't.

"Is it always like that?"

I grimace. "Sort of. Usually, I have my assistant or bodyguard with me, and if we go to the mall or somewhere out in the open, there's extra security around. I took a chance coming here, thinking everyone would assume I was on a tropical island nursing my broken heart."

"Is it broken?"

Turning toward Aiden, I glance up at him. Aiden squares his shoulders and his brows rise a fraction of an inch as I take him all in. He clears his throat, but doesn't look away from my heavy gaze, even as I move closer to him. "It isn't. I wasn't invested." I'm shocked by my admission, but it's true. In hindsight, I know now that Trey was a blip in my life. My forever is still out there somewhere.

Aiden's hand cups my cheek. His strong fingers press into the back of my head, bringing me closer to him. My lips pucker, waiting eagerly for his to press against mine.

"Can I help you find anything?"

Aiden and I jump back from each other. It's not that we were doing anything wrong, except we're in a children's store and kissing in public is definitely frowned upon. The repercussions would be too much, especially for Aiden. The last thing I want is for the media to hound Aiden and Holly, or dig into his past.

We spend the next hour or so shopping for Holly. Aiden let's me pick out most everything, but I make sure he's okay with it. I do spot a fairy princess nightgown set that has matching slippers that I'd like to buy for Holly, but I want to check with my mom first to make sure Aiden would be open to Holly receiving a gift from me.

By the time I'm done with what I need and his arms are loaded with not only my bags, but his as well, it's pitch black outside. Aiden walks me to my car and helps me get everything situated. "You know, had I known you were coming shopping we could've easily ridden together."

"Had I known you were coming, I would've given you my list and stayed at work," he says playfully.

"I had a lot fun today, Fish."

"Me too, Laney. And I get to tell Holly that I saved you today."

I laugh. "Yeah, you do. She'll think her father is a real hero." *At least he is to me.*

Aiden pulls me into his arms. His embrace is warm, friendly... too friendly. I thought that after our almost kiss he would try again, but he's kept his distance. I get it, though. I'd probably be the same way if I had lost my spouse. Some loves you never get over. When he pulls away I smile, hoping to convey my gratitude.

"So I guess I'll see you around."

"Probably," he says with a grin. "Ramona Falls is small. I'm bound to pull you over again."

I punch him lightly on his shoulder and he cowers.

"Seriously, though. Think about directing the school play for the festival. I know it's only a few weeks away, but the kids would love it."

"See ya, Fish." I get into my car, purposely ignore his comment regarding the play. As much as I'd love to do it, I can't march into the school and ask that I be given the responsibility. I'm sure they already have people to make sure everything goes off without any complications.

Aiden shuts my door and waves as I pull out of the spot. My head is swirling, thinking about missed connections with him. Would he have followed me to Los Angeles if we were still dating? It seems unlikely. We had only been together a few months, half a year or so if we had made it to graduation. That's not enough time for someone to make a life changing decision. If he would've asked me to stay, I would've told him no.

On my way, I decide to call Mindy. I'm eager to see her and spend some time with her family. I haven't been the best friend, letting my career consume my life, but I have sent her children gifts and did buy something for them today.

"Sup?" she asks.

"I can't believe that's how you answer the phone."

"Eh, I knew it was you. I suppose I could've been like OH EM GEE it's Delaney Du Luca!"

"Brat."

"I know. What's up?"

"Nothing," I tell her. "I'm driving back from the mall. I had to get some clothes, picked up a few presents, and happened to spend the day with Fish." I mumble the last part, unsure of how she'll react.

"Hold up. Did you say fish? As in Aiden Fisher?"

"Uh huh. Mindy, I think I like him."

"Wow... I just... wow... You know what? Good for you. Good for him."

"What do you mean?"

Mindy adjusts her phone and it sounds like she closes a door. "Sorry, I don't want Joel to hear. Did you know they're working together?"

"No, I didn't know Joel was a police officer. When did that happen?"

"A few years back. He wasn't happy at the bank so he took the test and went to the academy. He's happy, but moody. Anyway, Aiden's vulnerable, Delaney. His wife died and he's raising Holly by himself. We did some fundraisers for him to help offset the medical expenses insurance wouldn't pick up, but he's struggling. His house is falling apart. Joel and a few of the guys offered to help him fix it up, but he blows everyone off."

The more Mindy talks about Aiden, the more today makes sense. At lunch earlier he wanted to order chips and he made a face at anything I picked out over twenty dollars. I thought it was because he didn't like my taste, but if the man's broke, I can easily see why he doesn't want to spend money.

"Min, is Aiden broke?"

She sighs, and that's enough to tell me he is. "He's very proud, Delaney."

"I know. Listen, I gotta run. I have some calls to make,

but I want to come by and see you and the kids, maybe harass Joel for a bit, just let me know when, okay?"

"This weekend. Stop by on Saturday."

"I'll be there."

I hang up and drive the rest of the way home in silence. Everything about today makes complete sense. I just wish I had seen it sooner.

TEN

The presents I picked up for Holly sit tucked tightly away in my closet, hidden under garbage bags of clothes I have to do something with. I'm not looking forward to the day when I have to find creative ways to conceal any of her gifts. I know I made it hard for my parents and most of the time my mom would hide mine and Meredith's gifts in the car or attic where we didn't have access.

Standing back, I make sure everything looks normal before closing the door. I don't exactly expect Holly to come busting into my room to rifle through my closet, but a dad can never be too sure. I'm happy with what I was able to buy today, even with Delaney picking clothes and toys that were out of my budget.

When I was with her, I felt rather inadequate. She was spending money right and left, almost as if it grows on trees. I suppose for her, it does. I'll never know what that feeling is like though, and while it's not Laney's fault I'm in this predicament, I couldn't bring myself to tell her I live paycheck to paycheck, barely making ends meet. I had enough issues trying to maintain my composure. Being next to Delaney and trying to look at her as a friend and not a movie star was hard, but I think I managed not to make a complete fool out of myself.

The side door into the kitchen opens just as I step out into the hallway. The voices of Holly and my sister instantly fill the emptiness in my home. I miss the laughter that used to be here. The warmth of what having a wife felt like. When Heather found out she was sick, it was too late to do anything except make her comfortable. Overnight, everything changed. I had to be present. I had to make sure Holly made it to school, Heather made it to her appointments, and I had work. My life became about schedules, grocery shopping, paying bills. All things Heather had done for us. It took her getting sick for me to realize how much I took her for granted.

I clear my thoughts as soon as my eyes land on Holly. She looks tired as she staggers toward me. "Rough day?" I ask as she falls into me.

"You have no idea. The playground can be torture."

Meredith and I both laugh at her over exaggeration. "Well, I'm sure a nice long bath will ease all that tension away." I wish I were joking, but Holly has a penchant for bubble baths, much like her mother. If I don't set the timer, Holly will stay in until her skin rivals that of a ninety-year-old woman. "Why don't you go get your toys ready, and I'll be there in a few minutes to start the water."

"You got it. Bye Auntie Mere."

"Bye, sweetie. See you tomorrow."

As soon as Holly is down the hall, Meredith and I move into the kitchen. "Productive day?" she asks.

I nod and try to keep the smile off my face. The truth is, despite everything, I had a great time with Laney.

"No need to fill me in, I already heard you saved the day." My eyes go wide, and she shakes her head. "It's Delaney Du Luca, Aiden. She's one of the biggest stars out there and you, my brother, just happened to be her knight in shining armor." Meredith pokes me in the chest for emphasis. I drop my head to hide my smile, but I can't get anything past her. "Spill the details because the stuff I read all over the web is very outlandish."

"What'd you read?"

Instead of answering me, Meredith turns her attention to my refrigerator. I cringe as she opens it up. I half expect her to complain about the lack of food, but she doesn't. She hands me two beers before closing the door. I pop the tops of both and give one back to her. "Let's see, you were angry and told people to back off. A few comments said you showed your badge and pushed people out of the way."

I let those words stew for a bit while I take a long drink of my beer. Meredith does the same, but it's the way her eyes stay focused on me that I know I have no choice but to answer her. "Some of what you say could be true, but let me preface by saying, they were harassing her, and I was intervening long before I knew it was Delaney."

"She was just the prize behind the mob."

"Is that some intellectual metaphor I should know the meaning of?"

Meredith laughs. "Not at all. So, when are you taking Delaney out?"

The mouthful of beer I have sputters out of my mouth. My sister's eyebrow rises, making her look increasingly like our mother. "Never? She's Delaney Du Luca. She can have any man she wants, and I guarantee you I'm not on her radar."

"But she's on yours. Good night, brother." Meredith places her bottle down on the counter. I'm not sure she's even finished it, which bodes well in my favor. "Don't forget about my niece or Shelby."

"Shelby?" I ask.

"You're *definitely* on her radar." Meredith is out the door before I can even come close to giving a response. I lift the bottle of beer to my lips and replay the last bit of our conversation over in my head. I'm not in a position to be on anyone's mind, although dating wouldn't be a bad thing.

"Daddy!" Holly screeches, which causes me to go running. I burst into the bathroom to find her standing there in her bathrobe with her dolls lined up on the edge of the tub.

"What's wrong? Are you hurt?"

She looks at me oddly and shakes her head. "You told me to get ready for my bath."

"Right. I'm sorry, I forgot." I did because my mind was elsewhere, places it shouldn't be. Holly's my only priority in life right now. I kneel over and start the water, pouring the right amount of bubbles into the tub. I swear, whoever is lucky enough to marry my daughter better do this for her every night because she deserves it.

"I heard you saw my most favoritist person today."

"Favoritist isn't a word, Holly."

She shrugs and does nothing to correct herself, but continues to look at me as if I owe her something. "Who would that be?" I hedge. In my world, I should be her most favorite, but something tells me I'm not even on the list.

"Delaney," she says.

Right, of course. I nod and turn away from Holly so I

can shut off the water. "There ya go. I'll be in my room if you need me."

"Wait," she says, grabbing hold of my arm. "I'm dying to know."

That's when it hits me. My adolescent daughter transformed into a needy teenager while I was out shopping. Shouldn't she be worried about other things, like what time Frosty's on? "I'm not sure we have anything to discuss," I tell her as I stand there with my hands on my hips. She mimics my stance but does it with so much more flare.

"Dad," she says, drawing my name out in her whiny tone. "You were with her today. I heard all about it. Why can't you just tell me? Everyone in town says you saved her life."

"Your bath water is getting cold." I point to the tub of bubbles.

Holly sighs. "Fine, but once I'm in, you come sit on the toilet and talk to me."

This takes me by surprise, and as much as I'd rather not talk about today, I'm not going to pass up the opportunity to sit and talk with my daughter. I step out and wait by the door. It's seconds later when she hollers for me. When I walk back in, she's covered in bubbles and the only part of her visible is her head.

I sit on the toilet and sigh. I don't want her growing up so fast, but it seems inevitable. "Did you kiss her?"

"Holly!"

"What? She's very pretty."

"You can't go around kissing people. It's called harassment."

Holly rolls her eyes, making me second-guess my reason for being in here. I could try to change the subject but have a feeling she isn't going to stand for that. "Yes, Delaney is very pretty, and yes, I was with her today."

"Are you boyfriend and girlfriend?"

"No, why would you ask that?"

She shrugs. "Because Rachel said that Becky said Delaney was your girlfriend. Rachel made fun of me when I said it wasn't true and she said her mom told her and Rachel called me a baby for not knowing."

My mind is frazzled by the gossip these seven-year-olds participate in. I know it's not their fault, what they hear their parents talk about, but come on. Starting rumors where they aren't needed doesn't benefit anyone at all.

"Holly, you can't believe everything someone has to say." I almost add 'in this town', but refrain. "People like to make up stories so that they seem important or have information someone else doesn't have. Delaney and I are acquaintances. Do you know what that means?"

She nods. "You say hi, but don't invite them to dinner."

"Right, close enough. Today, Delaney was in trouble, so I helped her because it's my job to help people. That's the truth. Just because we were in the same spot at the same time doesn't mean we're dating."

"Do you want to date her?"

I shake my head. "Delaney lives in California. We live in Vermont. Now I'm going to leave you so you can have your bath. The timer's on, so wash up."

"Wait."

"What, Holly?"

"If you saved her today, that makes you her hero."

I nod and smile before stepping out of the bathroom and pulling the door closed until there's a small crack left. Within a few steps, I'm in my room and sitting on my bed doing everything I can to forget Holly's question about dating Delaney.

THE LOCKER next to me slams shut, causing me to jump. I'm half asleep, and the coffee I guzzled down on my way into work hasn't kicked in yet.

"Did you ever know that you're my hero...?"

Dominic's hand is outstretched as he continues to belt out the words to whatever song he's singing. I push his hand away and continue getting dressed.

"My sister was going on and on *and on* about the man who saved her," he says as he falls back into the row of lockers, placing his hand over his forehead in a very dramatic way.

"Whatever," I mumble.

"Seriously, though. As soon as Delaney came home, it was Aiden this and Aiden that. I wanted to plug my ears with glue so I wouldn't have to listen to her talk about you. It was like we were back in high school when she had those ridiculous puppy dog eyes for you. I used to sneak into her room to read her diary. She used to write Delaney Fisher all over the pages. Man, she took your break-up hard."

I keep my head down so Dominic can't see my expression. The reason we broke up was because he wouldn't stop teasing us. Delaney and I could never be alone, and when we were, he would interrupt us.

"You listening?"

"Yeah," I say, as I start to tie my boot.

"Anyway, I thought you should know she's back at it."

"I'm sure she was just experiencing some post-traumatic stress and needed to talk to someone about the incident."

Dom slams his locker door shut, causing me to jump again. "Nah, I think she has a crush."

I don't move a muscle until the door to the locker room shuts. It's only then that I allow myself to think about what Dom said, what Meredith said to me last night and what Holly told me. If things were different, I'd probably ask Delaney out, but her and I live in two completely different worlds.

ELEVEN

"I can do this. I can do this." Somehow repeating a positive affirmation is supposed to calm my nerves about driving in the snow. I can't say if this is the case or not because my car is still idling in my parents' driveway. I thought about arranging for an Uber, but when I mentioned it to my father, he shook his head. Apparently, the state isn't keen on allowing such services, leaving me no choice but to drive in two feet of freshly fallen snow.

Each winter, when I was a child, I'd sit in the window and pray for so much snow, the district would have no choice but to cancel school. The thought of staying home and putting on a play with my stuffed animals was more exciting then sitting through math class to learn multiplication – something I knew I'd never use in my profession. I can't recall one time a director has asked me to solve a math problem.

Somehow, Mother Nature never heard my prayers. Sure, the snow would fall, but school was never canceled, unless the roads were too icy. Too much ice meant everyone in our house stayed home and I was unable to hone my acting skills.

Acting and living in Los Angeles doesn't prepare you for driving in the snow or being able to see through rapidly moving wipers. I should stay home, but this is my now or never moment. Ever since Aiden mentioned the festival play, I can't seem to get it off my mind. I'm not sure if directing is what I want, but I do know I want to be involved. I want to give back to the community for all their support.

My knuckles are white from the tight grip I have on my steering wheel. Navigating unplowed roads is a nightmare and something I haven't done in ten years. I miss Calvin, my bodyguard who doubles as my driver when I'm not on set. After the incident at the mall, it's apparent I need him here. I should've known better than to think I could roam around without being noticed.

However, Aiden was there to save the day, and he's the reason I'm driving through this storm. All because he planted an idea in my head that won't go away. I don't know if the drama club needs or wants my help, but I'm going to volunteer anyway.

By the time I reach the main roads, they're at least drivable and I'm able to relax. At the stop sign, I shake my hands out and flex my fingers, bringing some life back to them. Across from me, a police car is parked along the snow bank. It's easy to see someone is in there, but I can't tell who. I'm tempted to pull along the side and see if it's Aiden or Dominic, but don't want to bother either of them at work. Yet, I'm tempted to show up just to torment Dom and maybe spill a few adolescent secrets to Eileen. I'm really looking forward to spending more time with her, to get to know her better, especially if she's going to my sister-in-law.

I honk and wave as I turn onto the road in case it's Aiden or my brother. Only a few more blocks and I'll be back at the school that opened my mind to acting. One simple school play, and I was bitten by the bug that would become my career. Funnily enough, I still remember the words to *Little Red Riding Hood*, my first lead.

Thankfully, there's a parking spot somewhat near the building, but between the slush, puddles and falling snow, my pants have water spots, my boots are dirty and my face is wet. I call this a win for the day, even though others may disagree. I think things could always be worse, like being dumped publicly by my B-list boyfriend who can't land a lead role.

The entryway of the school is as cold as I remember. Back when I was here, I used to run through this ice-cold space and into the warmth of the school. Dominic and I were two of the lucky kids because our parents drove us every day. I try the handle, but the door doesn't budge. I pull again, only to have the same result. The sign on the door tells me I have to push the button.

"What button?" I mutter to myself as I look for something to press.

"It's on the wall," a voice says, echoing through the corridor.

"Since you see me standing here, can't you just let me in?" I ask. There's a long silence until I hear the door click. I resist rolling my eyes as I paste a smile on my face. The woman behind the Plexiglas grins from ear to ear, no doubt realizing who I am.

"You're Delaney Du Luca, the Sweetheart of Ramona Falls."

Thanks. "Oh, I don't know about that."

"What, that you're Delaney? Have you fallen and hit

your head? Do you need me to call your parents?" the woman asks.

Only in a small town. "No, the sweetheart part. I'm sure there are other more deserving people than I am."

She shakes her head.

"Anyway, is Mrs. Winters available?"

"Let me see." She sits down and picks up a phone, smiling at me while she waits for someone to pick up the other end. In hindsight, I should've called and made an appointment with her. Dropping by in the middle of the school day is so unprofessional. I can't believe I've done this.

"Yes, I said *the* Delaney Du Luca."

My name catches my attention, only to find the receptionist gawking at me. I try to smile, but it feels forced so I stop trying.

"Mrs. Winters is waiting for you in her classroom."

"Great, thank you." I head toward the hall where I remember her room being. Artwork from the students lines the hall and each bulletin board is decorated for the holidays with green garland and snowflakes. I remember making trees with cotton balls and construction paper. Art was my favorite subject in elementary school.

I knock on the wooden door and turn the handle. Mrs. Winters turns her attention toward me as I step into her class. The loud gasps bring a wide smile to my face. I wave at her students and rush over to give her a hug. "It's so good to see you," I tell her.

Mrs. Winters pulls away, leaving her hands on my shoulders. "Look at you, Delaney, so grown up."

I nod and shrug. "You haven't changed one bit, Mrs. Winters."

"Just older," she says, brushing me off. She keeps her hand on my shoulder as she turns me to face the class.

"Children, allow me to introduce you to Delaney Du Luca."
I wave and everyone says hi. Most of the girls whisper
among themselves, and I find myself looking for Aiden's
daughter, even though I have no idea what she looks like
and the kids in this class seem to be older.

"I'm sorry to interrupt your class, Mrs. Winters."

"Oh no, worries. We were working on our songs for the
festival play."

"That's why I'm here. I'd like to help," I tell her,
watching as her eyes light up. She clasps her hands together.

"Oh, Delaney, I think that's just wonderful. Don't
you, class?"

The chorus of yesses gives me a surge of happiness. I
don't know why this means so much to me, but it does. Mrs.
Winters tells me there's a meeting after school and suggests
I be there. I promise her I will be before leaving her to tend
to her class.

With time to waste, I stop at the local diner and pick up
lunch to take to my favorite guy. Stepping inside my dad's
office is like stepping into a time machine. His walls are
covered with pictures of Dominic and me, from the time we
were toddlers until now.

My finger runs along the frames, each image bringing
up a good memory. The more time I seem to spend here, the
more I feel like I've been losing myself in Hollywood.
Everyone makes a big deal out of me being Delaney Du
Luca, when I really just want to be the girl who used to
follow her brother around, begging to play with him and his
friends.

"Well, aren't you a sight for sore eyes," my dad's voice
has me spinning on my heels to face him.

"Hi, Daddy." I hold up the greasy bag of food from
the diner.

"To what do I owe... oh no you didn't."

"I did, but only if you don't tell Mom!"

My dad rushes over to his door and peeks his head around the corner, asking his secretary to hold his calls. He shuts the door and rubs his hands together. "You can guarantee I won't tell your mom. Come on, let's sit."

He clears us off a spot on his table and holds the chair out for me. I rip into the bag of poutine and set it in the middle of the table. "I haven't had this since I left," I tell him, taking the first gravy drenched fry.

"No, I can't imagine poutine would be very popular in California."

My dad and I dig in. Every so often, our forks crash into each other, vying for that one soggy fry.

"Are you happy to be home?"

"I am. I still can't believe I ventured out in the storm today, though."

My dad looks out the window and laughs. "Storm? Sweetie, this isn't a storm."

I shrug. "It is to me. If there's even a hint of snow in Los Angeles, the town shuts down, the grocery stores are emptied and everyone hunkers down. It's like an apocalypse. I used to laugh, but now I do the same thing."

"I suppose people forget how to drive in the snow."

"And dress. I had to run to Burlington to buy clothes the other day."

Dad puts his fork down and rubs his belly. "I heard about that. Aiden saved the day?"

"He did. I think I'm going to call Calvin and ask him to fly out here. I thought I'd feel safe, but the other day..."

"You're popular, Delaney. People get excited when they see you. I don't think anyone will fault you for having your bodyguard with you. Maybe you should ask Dom to do it."

My eyes go wide at the suggestion of Dominic being my security detail. Something tells me he'd let someone get too close, thinking it's funny.

"Yeah, never mind," my dad says, laughing. "I have a feeling you and I just had the same thought."

"It's okay for Calvin to stay at the house?"

"Of course. He's family." Dad stands and comes over to me. He places a kiss on top of my head. "Duty calls though, sweetheart. I need to meet with the recreation committee about the festival."

"Speaking of, I stopped by and saw Mrs. Winters before I came here. I volunteered to help with the play. I thought it'd be a good way to give back to the community," I say, shrugging.

"Delaney, I think that's a great idea. I was going to ask if you'd be interested in doing a meet and greet during the festival? We can build a booth, set some time limits. I just know so many people are excited you're home and they all want to see you."

"Like a kissing booth?" I ask, winking at my dad. He turns red and it's not from embarrassment, but anger. The last thing he'd ever agree to is letting me have a kissing booth. I shrug. "It was worth a shot, but yes, I'll do a meet and greet for you."

"Thank you."

He comes back and pulls me from my seat so he can give me a hug. "I'm so happy you're home, Delaney. You've made this holiday even more special."

"Thank you, Daddy."

He sniffles as he pulls away, making sure I can't see if his face. Once he's out of sight, I start to clean up our lunch.

"He's happy you're home."

I look at the doorway to find a woman, whom I've never met, standing there. "Thanks. I'm happy to be here."

"I'm Shelby," she says, walking toward me with her hand extended. "I'm the chairwoman of the recreation committee."

"Nice to meet you." I try to juggle the trash as best as I can while trying to shake her hand. Unfortunately, the bag falls onto the floor, open side down. *Great, there's going to be gravy and cheese curds everywhere.* "Sorry about that."

"No worries. Anyway," Shelby says with a sigh. "It was nice to meet you." She waves as she leaves his office. I look down at the mess, only to see gravy running down the front of my pants.

"Lovely."

TWELVE

AIDEN

*H*oliday decorations line the street my parents live on. Everything from classic lights to a waving Frosty, and an inflatable Santa with a reindeer set haphazardly on a roof. People here don't spare any expense when it comes to bringing holiday cheer.

Pulling into my parents' driveway, my truck's pelted with snowballs immediately. I try to look for the culprit, but only see multiple shadows. Whoever is outside, they're leaving me no choice, but to sneak out of my truck. As stealthily as possible, I slide out, quickly realizing I'm not as young as I used to be. As luck would have it, my father plowed his driveway, leaving me without any ammunition to face my attackers. Thankfully, I'm a trained police officer and while I don't participate in tactical training, I did learn a few things at the academy.

The edge of the garage is only a few feet away; I hightail it as fast as I can, without slipping, until I'm safely behind the wall. The pile of snow, left over from the plow makes for the perfect barricade. I situate myself behind the bank, and start assembling my arsenal of snowballs. My enemy heckles me from across the yard. The only problem I can see is my truck being in the way. Had I known I was going to be ambushed, I would've parked on the street.

"We know you're out there," the voice of my dad yells out, followed by the tiniest of giggles. Of course, my daughter is on his side.

"You can't hide forever, Daddy—"

"No, don't call him that."

"I mean, yeti." Holly laughs again.

"Yeti?" I yell back. "How am I a yeti?" I ask, even though one look at me clearly proves I'm heading in the direction of full on yetiness with the amount of snow covering my legs right now.

Without any provocation from me, a snowball flies toward my direction. It only misses by a few inches, but the eminent danger I fear causes me to launch a counterattack. I throw three snow bombs back-to-back blindly into the night, hoping to hit either one of my targets. A round of giggles leads me to believe I completely missed Holly and my father.

"Incoming," my father yells. I make the mistake of looking up, only to be pelted with a hard packed ball to my face. My body falls to the ground, my back slamming against the cold, hard snow. The padding my jacket does nothing to soften my fall.

"Ugh," I say, wiping away the water remnants. I have no doubt there'll be a goose egg knot on my forehead within the next few minutes. Now that they know my location, I'm left with no choice but to forge ahead with an attack. I may not come out as victor, but I won't go down without a fight.

Making sure to cup my arm, I pile a mound of snowballs

in there. As quietly as I can, I sneak over to the other side of my truck and start throwing snow bombs into the bushes. The sound of my dad grunting changes my aim. I toss everything I have until I'm empty.

I move into the middle of the yard, knee deep in the snow and start my victory dance. My dad never shows his face, but his aim is on point when multiple balls head my way. More laughter rings out from behind the bushes, mostly little girl giggles.

"I give up," I say. "Mercy."

"Daddy, you can't quit."

"I'm out of ammo. I surrender."

Holly stands up, covered head to toe in snow. Only the lights strung above her and in the trees light the path toward her. I snatch her up and hug her tightly. When she pulls away, her cheeks are bright red and her nose is running. "Are you cold?"

"No, I'm having fun with grandma and grandpa."

"I see that." I set her down and turn toward the shrubs. "You can come out now, coward." My mouth drops open when I see my mother stand first, followed slowly by my father. "My whole family?"

"Meredith stayed inside."

"Well, it's nice to see my sister cares about me."

My mom shakes her head. "She didn't want to be cold," she says, shrugging.

I shake my head and look down at Holly. "This was your doing, right?"

Holly shrugs and makes the sweetest face possible. I'm tempted to push her into the snow bank, but instead I scoop her up and carry her into the garage so she can take off her snowsuit.

"Was that fun?" I ask her.

"The best. Grandpa and I made snowballs after school."

"Maybe next time you'll give your old man a warning."

"You're not old, Daddy."

I smile and kiss her on the nose before directing her inside. Holly and I go over to the woodstove to try to warm up. "Smells good," I holler toward the kitchen.

"Thanks." The voice is from someone familiar, but I can't picture who it is until Shelby comes around the corner. She rests against the small piece of wall separating the kitchen from the living room.

"Shelby," I say her name more out of shock than anything. I didn't see another car out there when I pulled in, not that I was looking for one, and can honestly say I wasn't expecting to see her at my parents'. She comes over to me, her stocking feet sliding across the hardwood floors. With both hands on my shoulders, she leans forward and kisses me on my cheek, lingering there for a minute. Holly reaches for my hand, tugging me away.

I smile softly at both of them, but have never been so thankful for Holly to want my attention. "I didn't know you were joining us for dinner."

"Meredith offered, said your parents wouldn't mind."

Unfortunately, Shelby's right, my parents won't mind even though they really can't afford to feed many more mouths. Both my parents work their fingers to their bones and Meredith shouldn't invite her friends to dinner.

"How was work?" she asks. Shelby motions for me to follow her to the sofa. I do so, not wanting to be rude. Holly comes with me and climbs up onto my lap.

"Work was... well, most of it was spent getting people out of ditches."

"We never learn, do we?"

"Learn what?" I ask.

"To slow down. To take corners easily. To just stop and pay attention to your surroundings."

Shelby's right. I chuckle. "You sound like a public service announcement."

She laughs, throws her head back and in the process her hand lands near my thigh. My legs still might be numb from the cold weather, but I can definitely feel her fingers press against my jeans. Her flirting isn't so subtle.

"Public service is what I do best," she says, moving closer. "If you want, I can find you something to do for the winter festival. I'm working hand-in-hand with the mayor to make it the best one yet."

My parents walk into the living room with a tray of mugs. Holly bolts from my lap to go retrieve her cup of what I'm assuming is hot cocoa.

"Shelby, would you like some?" my mother asks.

"Yes please, Mrs. Fisher. Meredith has raved about your homemade cocoa. I've been dying to try it." She takes a cup from my mother and instead of keeping it for herself, she hands it to me and reaches for another one. Holly follows my mom back to the kitchen, where the banging of pots and pans becomes a bit louder.

"Thanks," I say, giving her a half smile. "Where's Shawna?" I ask after noticing she's not here.

"She's with her father. He's in town for the night and asked to see her." Shelby breaks eye contact with me and looks down at her mug.

Ever since Meredith started talking about Shelby, I've never considered where her ex-husband is or was. Nor have I asked because I didn't think it was my business. I'm sure if I listen hard enough around town, the gossipmongers will no doubt fill me in about Shelby. Thing is, I'm interested... sort of. I'm not sure I'm ready to date or maybe I'm not positive she's the one I want to date. Yes, it'd be nice because our daughters are the same age. Yes, Shelby is beautiful. However, I feel like there should be a spark. I haven't felt that... yet. "For the night?"

Her thumb moves up and down the side of her cup. I tear my eyes away from there to focus on her, giving her my undivided attention. "We divorced last year. Shawna and I moved here to start over and he stayed in the city."

"New York?" I ask.

She nods. "His job requires him to travel. I used to go with him until Shawna started school. We thought it would be better that I stay home so her schedule wasn't interrupted and she wasn't raised by the nanny. As with any cliché, he started having... well, he just wasn't a very good husband to me and that led to a lot of fighting. We tried counseling, bought a house here with the intent he'd quit his job and we'd live here, but someone else was more important to him."

"But he's a good dad?"

Shelby shakes her head. "I wish. I can deal with him letting me down, but not Shawna. She really doesn't understand why he's never around. He tells her it's because of work, but he brought his new girlfriend to Vermont to ski. I guess he thought he'd introduce Shawna to her. I didn't really ask him when he called this morning to let me know he wanted to see her." She shrugs. "I can't really tell him no because the court order allows for visitation and he pays his child support. Nor does he listen when I tell him how much he's hurting her when he doesn't come to visit or call. He thinks he's doing the right thing by staying gone all the time, says daughters need their mothers while growing up."

I thought I had it bad. I don't know how I would react if Heather had decided the life we were sharing wasn't what she wanted and only came around sporadically to see Holly. Maybe in a sense abandonment would be better than death, but then again, maybe not. I also can't imagine not being a part of Holly's life, and I'm not sure how any parent ever comes to the conclusion their child is better off without them.

"I'm sorry, Shelby."

She smiles back in kind. "It's not easy being a single parent."

I half scoff half laugh. "No, it's definitely not." I've had my doubts about my ability to parent since Heather passed away. I often lie in bed at night, wondering what I'm doing and how many ways I am messing up Holly's life, but then I look at her and see the way she needs me and my hectic crazy life seems to make sense for the most part. As easy as it would be to walk away from my life, it'd be the hardest decision to make.

"You know Meredith has offered to babysit if you and I wanted to grab dinner some night."

Nothing like being caught off guard. I take a drink of my hot cocoa and try to form an answer. I haven't wanted to date at all, and I'm still not sure I do, but maybe I have to get back out there.

"We'll have to take her up on her offer some day." *This* apparently is the right thing to say because Shelby smiles brightly.

"I'd like that, Aiden."

Shelby starts to move closer just as my mom lets us know dinner is ready. I move so fast, I'm sure Shelby probably toppled over. That thought alone brings a grin to my lips, even though it's far from funny.

At the table, she chooses to sit next to me. Her thigh rests against mine and while I'm tempted to ask her to give me some space, I don't. However, I do knock my sister's water over, soaking her lap. I've told her before, I'm not interested in dating, yet my words haven't sunk in. I may have agreed to go on a date with Shelby, but I feel like she's being stuffed down my throat, and that's because my sister is a meddler.

THIRTEEN

DELANEY

*T*he one thing I haven't been able to do in my career is sing. Not because the opportunities haven't presented themselves, but because I can't carry a tune. I'm the world's best singer in the shower, my car and even when I'm home alone and no one is around to hear me. I've been known to belt out a song or two with my friends in the car, despite the volume always seeming to be turned up louder. If that's a sign I shouldn't, I always miss it because in my mind, I'm *that* great. Ask anyone of my friends and they'll tell you otherwise. I'm tone deaf, a lyrical screecher with a voice so bad I can break a vase. Not literally, but it's been implied.

The sheet music reads like a jumbled mess. I don't remember a thing from choir and each time Mrs. Winters looks over at me, I smile and continue to make my mouth move. Thankfully, the fifth grader I'm standing next to sings like Pavarotti and he's making me sound amazing. Honestly, I'm not sure why Mrs. Winters has me standing with the choir because I won't be performing, at least, I hope that's not her plan.

When her hands finally come to rest, I drop my sheet music and move back to the other side of the room while she speaks with the students. "Let's close the risers and get into character. Ms. Du Luca is going to take over from here."

Finally, I think as I grab the script from my bag. I have it memorized, with each part tabbed with a different colored flag. I stayed up all night, reading and making slight changes, wanting this to be perfect.

Standing in front of a couple dozen students, all staring back at me, is worse than a stressful audition. Each one is focused, waiting for me to say something or stumble and fall on my face. No, they wouldn't want that, right? I swallow hard, clear my throat and inhale deeply as if I've never breathed in before. I smile, but it feels weak, forced even, as most of the students keep me pinned under their watchful gaze.

The young Pavarotti raises his hand. I nod and squeak out a measly, "yes."

"My father says with you directing our play, people from all walks of life will be at the festival."

All walks of life? What does that even mean?

"Tell your father thank you." *I think.* "Okay, if I could have Betsy and Michael come forward, we'll get started." I read from the cast list Mrs. Winters has provided for me. When the students step forward, I feel a sense of relief. I don't know if it's because they're here or if it's because I'm really doing this. I'm going to help direct the winter play.

The play we're doing is one Mrs. Winters wrote. It's about a young child who is adamant his parents choose the smallest tree with as few branches as possible, after hearing the tree farmer is going to chop it down and turn it into mulch. Of course, his parents want the big full tree, but the young boy is determined.

"Betsy, if you'll take it from page one, and Michael you'll follow right after."

"We know, Ms. Du Luca, we were practicing before you arrived," Betsy says. I nod and bite my tongue from the harsh response that's sitting there. No need for snark is what I want to say. Instead, I motion her to start. *Actresses!*

Throughout the hour, children come and go for rehearsal. It won't be until a night or two before the festival when the cast will be together. Mrs. Winters says children are so busy these days, getting them to volunteer for school functions has become harder and harder, until she implemented the winter play into the choir program and held tryouts for those not in her class. Still some students have other activities, which makes it difficult. Back when Dominic and I were in school, our parents made sure we stayed active, but committed.

When the last round of elementary students strolls in, the tiny gasps get my attention quickly. Two girls are huddled together and not hiding the fact that they're pointing at me. I wave, which starts a round of giggles.

I go to them and crouch down. "What are your names?" I ask.

"I'm Shawna and this is my bestie, Holly, but she's shy."

Holly... Aiden's Holly. I can tell immediately it's her. I don't know if it's because she's Aiden's daughter or if it's because of the way her blue eyes sparkle, but I'm completely taken by her. There's something about her that reminds me of myself when I was her age. My hand immediately goes out and Shawna shakes it. Holly is hesitant, but eventually sets her small hand into mine. "Hi Holly, I'm Delaney."

Once I get the younger kids situated, we practice their songs and stage placement. For the most part, they will be in the background singing, holding and even being props, and a few will have a line or two. Fortunately, Mrs. Winters has already chosen who will speak. I say this because I already know I'd play favorites and pick Aiden's daughter, which already makes me a crappy director.

After fifty minutes of practice, the bell finally rings. Everyone lines up at the door, waiting for their teacher to come back. When the last child is out, I slump in the chair. "That was exhausting."

"Says the actress who does this for eighteen hours a day," Mrs. Winters points out with a laugh.

"It's not the same. I get breaks every few takes. A nap if I want one. Food when I need it. I can walk off set and use the restroom even though the director will get angry; they can't really say anything to me. But here—"

"Here is different. Here means always being on your best behavior even when a child is telling you 'all walks of life will be in town.'"

"What did he mean?" I ask her.

Mrs. Winters sits down next to me and pats my leg. "I suppose your parents stay quiet on the town gossip, although with you being back, I'm surprised you haven't run into Leo's parents."

I chuckle at his name. It's wrong and unprofessional, but considering I called him Pavarotti, I can't help it. "Honestly, they try to shelter me from everything, especially since my father became mayor."

"As I suspected. Leo's father ran against your dad a few times. He's determined to unseat him."

"And his father thinks I'm going to what, bring the degenerates out?"

She shrugs. "Doesn't matter what his father thinks. Everyone in Ramona Falls is happy you're home. I heard you'll have a booth at the festival." She looks at me with a gleeful smile.

"I tried for a kissing booth, but he wouldn't go for it." We both laugh. Even when I suggested it, I knew it'd be a long shot. "You know, that was the first time my dad ever asked me to do something like that; use my career in such a way."

"How'd you feel?"

I shrug. "Oddly, I don't seem to care."

THE DRIVE to the airport took longer than expected, and by the time I pull in I don't have to park because Calvin is already standing outside. He's six foot five and sticks out like a sore thumb. I park along the curb and hop out, running up to him. "I'm so sorry I'm late. The roads were crap and I had to drive slowly." My arms try to wrap around his waist, but the truth is, he's like ten times my size.

"It's cold here."

No, hi Delaney or boss lady.

"Really?"

Calvin chuckles, but ignores me as he sets his bags into the back and instantly climbs into the driver's seat. I fist pump, earning an odd look from the police officer who is standing by one of the two entrances with his head on a swivel, watching people go in and come out of the terminal. He probably doesn't realize how happy I am to give up driving duties.

"We need something bigger," he says as I slip into the passenger side of the car and buckle up. He puts the car into drive, but instead of leaving the area, he pulls into the parking garage and turns toward the rental return area.

"What are you doing?"

"Upgrading. I can't drive around in this... sardine can."

"It's not *that* bad," I say.

Calvin glares at me before getting out of the car. In a matter of minutes, Calvin has my cute little car emptied, keys turned in and us sitting comfortably in an oversized SUV, complete with tinted windows. If people hadn't heard I was in town, they will now.

"Once you called, I made the arrangements to change the vehicles over," he tells me as he follows my directions to the interstate.

"I figured as much." I sigh and press the button to turn on the seat warmer. Truthfully, I'm happy to have something bigger, although I'd never be able to drive it. "I think you'll like Ramona Falls."

"Is it warmer?"

I laugh. "Nope, just as cold and we have a bunch of outside activities planned. We're going to go ice skating, maybe build an igloo, definitely make some snow angels, and we'll get you on a sled."

"Mhm," he hums.

"When's the last time you saw snow?" I ask him.

"Years. I'm not a fan."

"Neither am I." But I'm happy to be back in Ramona. There's something about being home that makes everything seem okay. To be honest, I haven't missed Los Angeles, aside from the weather. I definitely don't miss the fast paced life. "You know, I'm thinking of buying a property here."

"You just told me you don't like the snow," he points out.

"True, but I like the solitude. It's nice to drive down the road and know it'll only take you literally twenty minutes to get to the grocery store. The lack of traffic is nice, and people don't bother me here."

"So what happened at the mall that prompted you to call me?"

"That was different. I think if I had gone with someone, I would've been okay. My mistake was thinking no one would recognize me, let alone have the mob mentality once they did. I fully expected to sign a few autographs and pose for some selfies, but... Anyway, Aiden was there and he helped."

"The ex boyfriend?" Calvin glances at me and waggles his eyebrows.

I roll my eyes. "Sometimes I wish I had never introduced you to my brother. I swear you both are worse than women with your gossip."

Calvin laughs. "It's not gossip when he's informing me you were accosted at the mall. If you hadn't called, I would've shown up anyway."

"You deserve a vacation, Calvin. And time with your family."

He smiles. "You're my family, Delaney. And it's my job to protect you."

I reach across the console and hug his bicep. I feel bad I'm tearing him away from his parents during the holidays, and fully intended to give him a month off. "While you're here, I have a few things to do. One of them is the booth, as you know, but I'm also helping out with the festival play. I know Dom wants to spend time with you. He talked about taking you to Boston for a Celtics or Bruins game."

"That'll be fun."

"Other than that, it's mostly hanging out at my parents' and strolling around town."

"No singing Christmas carols, right?"

"You've heard me sing. Do you honestly think I'll subject my parents' neighbors to my voice?"

Calvin shrugs. "You force me to listen all the time."

"You're paid to listen, buddy. I don't want the neighbors running into their homes when they see me outside. You can guarantee, there will be no going door to door for any of us."

"Phew, what a relief."

I swat him in his arm, but he only laughs. He signals to exit and follows my instructions on how to get to Ramona Falls. When he turns onto Main Street, his mouth drops open in amazement. Garlands, white lights and red ribbons decorate every wrought iron light pole along the street. Every store has a holiday display and if he were turn the radio off, he'd hear music playing from the speakers set up outside.

"This is like something out of a book or movie."

"It's pretty special," I tell him. The town looks like a Norman Rockwell painting came to life.

FOURTEEN

AIDEN

*I*t's been a few days since I've had any run-ins with Delaney and I'm sensing since her friend from Los Angeles is here, she's stopped talking about me, as my locker hasn't been decorated nor has Dominic sang to me. Honestly, I miss the teasing. Not because I enjoy being harassed by Dom, but because until Delaney's return, my friend has walked on eggshells where I've been concerned and it's nice to see him getting back to his old self. I suppose I have Delaney to thank for that.

Dominic storms into the locker room, fully dressed and ready to go for the day. He sets his foot on the bench, resting his forearm on his thigh. "What're you doing after work?"

"Eating, sleeping, sanding my floors, homework. The list is endless when I get home. Why, what's up?"

"D scored some tickets to the Bruins game tonight. Wanna go? Eileen can watch Holly."

I do want to go. It's been entirely too long since I've been out with the guys. When Heather became ill, our lives changed. They had to. Friends are there, but relationships take a backseat. Unfortunately, hockey tickets are expensive and there's no way I can afford them. I start to shake my head, but his hand goes up.

"I wasn't clear," he says as he pulls out his phone. He clicks a few times before he hands it to me. On the screen are his messages with his sister.

Delaney: I have four tickets to the Bruins tonight.

Dominic: For me?

Delaney: For you, Calvin, Dad and Fish.

Dominic: Does Fisher know?

Delaney: Nope. Figured you can tell him or I can ☺

I hand Dominic his phone back without saying anything. I don't want the handout, but it's nice she's thinking about me.

"As you can see, it's non-negotiable. I mean, I could call my sister and have her talk to you."

"No need," I tell him as I shut my locker. "I'll have to see if my mom can take Holly." Thing is, I already know she can. It's Friday night and Holly often spends the night there so I can pretend to do something around the house, when really all I do is look through our photo albums because I fear I'm going to forget the smallest of details about Heather.

"Like I said, Eileen will watch her or I'm sure D wouldn't mind."

"I'm not pawning my daughter off on your sister. Besides, if they were to leave and have another incident at the mall, I don't think I'd be able to forgive myself."

"My sister would protect Holly, Fisher. You have to know that."

I nod. "And who would protect your sister?"

Dominic drops his foot from the bench and stands tall. "You're right." He pats me on the back and leaves his hand there until we're at the door. "Calvin is going to drive. Delaney says we can take her rental."

"Her car? No way can the four of us fit in there."

Dom laughs. "Calvin rented an SUV when he arrived. It's completely decked out. We'll be riding in luxury." Dominic heads into the station without realizing the weight of his words. Luxury... something I don't have and can only experience when others take pity on me. It's not that I think Delaney is taking pity, but it feels like it.

Living in a small town has its benefits along with its drawbacks. One of the perks is I don't have to have a partner when I'm on patrol. I suppose being alone all day could make my day seem boring, but it's not. I like the flexibility of eating when I want, stopping when I need to or hanging out at the station when the chief is in a good mood. The drawback is everyone knows your business.

By the time I park my car and get out, people are telling me how jealous they are that I'm going to watch the Bruins tonight. I swear it hasn't been ten minutes since Dominic asked me, and yet people already know. And when I step into the diner, after the bells have stop chiming, three others make comments.

"News travels fast, sweetheart," Wanda says as I take a seat at the counter. She pours me a cup of coffee. On weekdays, I can come for breakfast and eat for under five dollars. This diner has been around since the early nineteen hundreds and has been in the same family the entire time. A fire once threatened it, but the town folks came out in droves to help the local volunteer firefighters extinguish the flames before they did too much damage.

"How come when someone commits a crime, people don't know who did it before we do?"

"Dunno, sugar. Maybe we only like to chatter about the good stuff."

That has to be it because we all know mums the word when we're trying to find who stole a bike, smashed a mailbox or stole an inflatable snowman out of the Smiths' yard. Wanda sets my breakfast down, but doesn't leave a bill. "Where's the check?" I ask. She points toward the other side of the restaurant, where Delaney is sitting, watching me. Delaney motions for me to join her. I hesitate for a moment before picking up my plate and cup of coffee.

The tables I pass say hello, and one even makes a comment about me joining Delaney for breakfast.

"You picked up my tab," I say as I sit down.

"I saw you sitting there and thought, why not."

"Because I'm capable of taking care of my own checks," I tell her. Immediately, I realize how harsh my words are and shake my head. "I didn't mean it like that. It just, first lunch the other day, the hockey ticket this morning and now this."

"I didn't mean anything—"

I hold up my hand in a silent plea for her to stop. I don't want her apologies, not when I owe her one. "I'm sorry for what I said, Laney. I'm not used to people looking out for me. Not since Heather died."

"That's how it works, right? When people get sick or die, others come out and help. They make food for weeks, they stop by and make sure everything is okay, and then it all stops. Everything you became dependent on disappears rather quickly."

I look at her for a moment, wondering how she knows

this. Everyone in her family is still alive and as far as I can remember, she's never dealt with a loss of any magnitude. "Did you play a widow in a movie?"

"No, Mindy's father died when we were in high school. I was there. I remember her mother saying something one time. I imagine it's the same, right?"

"Why are we talking about this?" I ask.

Delaney leans back against the booth and shakes her head. "I don't know. We can change the subject. I met your daughter yesterday."

"You did? Where?"

"At school. I'm helping Mrs. Winters with the festival play, just like you suggested."

I can feel my cheeks getting higher and higher as my smile becomes wider. "That's great. I'm sure the students will love having you on board, especially Holly, although I'm surprised she didn't say anything to me about meeting you."

"Maybe she's not as big of a fan as you thought."

"No, that's definitely not the case." I use this opportunity to finally take a bite of my breakfast. Wanda comes by to refill our coffee and drop off Laney's order of pancakes, no syrup but with whipped cream. Wanda doesn't stay to chat or ask if we need anything else before she's barking orders.

"Still putting whipped cream on your pancakes?"

Delaney nods as she sticks a fork full into her mouth. Her eyes close as her lips wrap around the fork. "So good," she mumbles with her mouthful. After she swallows, she points her fork at me. "You know, I like being home in Ramona Falls."

"Why's that?"

"Because no one cares that I'm here. I mean look around, this place is packed and yet not a single person... oh wait that guy is staring, but still."

I turn and look at the man she's referring to. I haven't seen him around before, which does seem odd since I know everyone in town. It's clear he's not from around here and by the looks of it, he's alone. "People care, Laney. They respect your privacy." Even as I say it, I'm not sure they do. "Where's your bodyguard?"

"Calvin?"

I nod, wanting to know why she's alone. Not that I can't protect her, but she does pay someone to do it.

"He's running."

"In the snow?"

Delaney laughs. "I know, I couldn't believe it when he said he was going, but he laced up and took to the streets. I have a feeling he's going to fall and hurt himself."

"Well, I hope not because Dom said he's driving us to Boston in your fancy new rental. You know, if you had that to begin with you probably wouldn't have been pulled over for speeding." I wink at her. She covers her face with her hands, but not before I witness her cheeks turning pink.

"You should've never pulled her over to begin with. Honestly, Aiden, what were you thinking?" Wanda asks, shaking her head. She sets her empty glass coffee pot down on the table and places her hands on her hips. I half expect her to waggle her finger at me as if she's scolding me. Still, I do the only thing I can think of and point to Delaney.

"She was speeding and talking on her cell phone, Wanda. If it had been anyone else, the town would be in an uproar. You know it and so does everyone else. I can't choose who I pull over based on their career."

"He has a point, Wanda. I *was* breaking the law," Delaney says in my defense.

"Thank you," I say.

"Oh, that doesn't mean I forgive you because I don't."

I throw my hands up in the air. Both Delaney and Wanda start to laugh. "Women," I mutter, only to hear a "here, here," coming from another booth. I give a thumb up to whoever is supporting me right now.

Wanda goes over to Delaney and puts her arm around her shoulder. "It's just because we haven't had her home in such a long time, and you had to give her a rude welcoming."

Laney crosses her arms over her chest and gives me a smirk. I toss my napkin down on the table. "What can I do to make it up to the both of you?" I ask, pleading for some mercy.

Both women look at each other for a moment before Wanda opens her mouth. "I think you need to take Delaney here out to dinner."

"Um..."

"Don't um me, mister. What's said is done, now make the plans before I make them for you." Wanda takes her pot and starts hollering something to one of the cooks. Delaney and I look at each other, neither of us saying anything. The problem is, everyone else in the restaurant is looking at us as well.

I clear my throat, wondering how I'm going to get out of this. It's not that I don't want to take her out. It's more along the lines that I can't give her what she's used to. "I know you're used to fancy—" I'm interrupted by the screeching sound of my radio. "This is 8 2 4."

"We have a situation over at the clinic and your assistance is needed," Eileen says.

"Roger that, I'll be there in five." I toss some money down on the table, not caring that Delaney has already paid for my breakfast. "I'll talk to you later, Laney," I say as I hustle out of the diner. The call couldn't have come any sooner. I'm so far out of Delaney Du Luca's league, it saved me from making a fool out of myself.

FIFTEEN

DELANEY

*F*or the first time in a long time, I'm laughing. It's a full-on belly laugh with achy sides and shortness of breath. It's genuine and heartfelt. It's being done without effort or a conscious decision to make sure I look my best for a camera. I don't care if there are Santa's on my leggings or that Rudolph's nose lights up on my sweatshirt. I finally feel free from the restraints of Hollywood.

We're in a lounge in New Hampshire, which is a short drive from Ramona Falls, and the ambiance alone is worth it. With the guys in Boston for hockey, it left us women all alone. Sure, we could've gone shopping or wrapped presents, but this is better. It's nicer, and we can hang out.

When we first walked in, very few people recognized me. Of course, I'm trying to throw people off by my attire because what self-respecting actress would be caught dead, out in public, with an ugly Christmas sweater on? This one! But now that we've moved from the restaurant to the lounge, people are watching. They're documenting my every move with their cell phones and undoubtedly blasting my actions all over social media. I'm half tempted to find them all and comment, but I won't. Doing so gives the privacy invaders the satisfaction they crave, and honestly, I'd rather read their friends' comments, especially those who disapprove of the post.

I think being home has brought this out of me, the ability to snort in a lounge full of people, in front of my friends and family, and not freak out. This feels good. This is how I should be all the time.

"Thanks, Mom." I put my arm around my mother and pull her close to me, kissing her on the cheek. She stays there for a brief moment before pulling away to look at me. If I'm not mistaken, there are a few unshed tears in her eyes. These are new, not the ones left over from one of our many laughing stints.

"For what?"

"For telling me to come home. I needed this," I tell her. She hugs me back, but it's different. It's like she needed me too.

"Astrid and Delaney, look at me." My mom and I turn our heads at the sound of Mindy's voice. Her phone is out, and she snaps the picture instantly. "I have a few others too," she says as she sits down to show us. Mindy flips through her camera roll, showing us the images she's taken. They're of my mom and I hugging, looking at the camera, but my favorite is the one of us looking into each other's eyes. I can see how proud my mom is of me and I hope that she knows how much I love her.

"Can you send these to me?" I ask Mindy.

"Of course, what else would I do with them?"

I shake my head and smile softly at her. "Nothing. I know you'd never do anything to betray my trust."

Mindy pulls me into a hug. I squeeze her tightly. It's my way of showing her how much I appreciate her, even when

I haven't been the best of friends. Hollywood changes people. The constant rush of life is exhausting. When I arrived in Los Angeles, I submerged myself in work, reading scripts, going to auditions and social engagements, and forgetting about everyone back home. If it weren't for my parents calling and texting constantly, I likely would've lost them due to my inability to see past the haze I buried myself in.

"Thank you for coming out tonight. I know it was short notice."

"Like I would miss this." Mindy spreads an arm out over the crowd. There's a line of men sitting on stools with their backs facing the bar. Each one is watching my little group and trying to flirt with us. Their smoldering, borderline constipation, eye squint is on point.

"This is nothing. You should come out to LA sometime. My treat, of course. I'll show you around. Introduce you to a few of the players. We can go to Malibu and sit on the beach. We'll hit up a fancy nightclub and dance all night."

"Sound amazing, but—"

"I know, the kids make it hard. We can make it a family vacation and do Disneyland or something."

"What's gotten into you?" she asks. "Since when are kids your thing?"

Her question gives me pause. Throughout my career, I've been adamant about children not being a part of life. I don't want to be an absent mother or have my child raised by nannies. My colleagues are like that, and it's bothered me ever since I took my first starring role.

"I don't know," I tell Mindy. "Maybe it's being home and working with the students on the play?" I don't know why I'm questioning myself. It's not like I have the answer.

"Maybe it's from spending some quality time with a

certain single dad?" Eileen chimes in. Instantly I feel flushed and find myself bowing my head to hide.

"Aiden?" my mom asks. "You've been spending time with Aiden?"

"No," I say in defense. Not that spending time with Aiden is a bad thing. "I was at the diner this morning, and he was there. I invited him to sit with me. It's not like we're secretly meeting up at night."

"Why not?" Mindy asks. When I look at her, she shrugs and picks up her drink.

"Oh come on," I say, pushing softly against her shoulder. "The last thing I need is another romance. Nope, Delaney Du Luca is single, and she's going to stay that way for a long time."

My mom scoffs and rolls her eyes. "Aiden would make a fine boyfriend."

"Yeah maybe, if I didn't live thousands of miles away and work eighteen hour days."

"So you admit you like him?" Eileen asks, waggling her eyebrows before she starts laughing.

I throw my napkin at her. "You're not listening to me. I don't have time for a boyfriend." I purposely avoid her question. I do like Aiden; I wouldn't want to ruin his life by being mixed up in mine. It wouldn't be fair to him or Holly.

"Oh, I think we hear you loud and clear," Mindy says.

Shaking my head. "You ladies are incorrigible and exactly why rumors start. It was breakfast, nothing more."

"And hockey tickets," Eileen adds.

"Because Calvin will be bored here. I wanted him to bond with the guys."

"Sure ya did, honey." My mom pats me on the back of my leg as I pass by her.

"Mindy's right. Aiden needs a woman like you," Eileen adds.

"Mom, a little help here?" I beg.

"Sorry, Delaney, I have nothing. I agree with the girls."

I throw my hands up in the air and fall back against the sofa. "You all are just... well I don't know what you are, but come on. The last thing Aiden wants or needs in his life is me."

"Why would you say something like that? Has Aiden told you what he needs?" my mom deadpans.

"Look, we had breakfast, nothing more. I called him over to my table because he was by himself and I was alone. I don't understand why everyone looks for a hidden meaning when there isn't one. A long time ago, in a land far far away, Aiden and I were a couple... but that was back in high school. I left. He got married and had a daughter. It's not like either of us has spent years pining away for each other." I look at my mom, future sister-in-law and my best friend. Each of them has a smirk on their faces, which boggles my mind. I'm either incredibly dense, or they're up to something. Shaking my head, I get up and head toward the bar, taking the first stool available. I sigh heavily and raise my finger to get the attention of the bartender.

"Sounds like a heated conversation," the man next to me says. I close my eyes and nod.

"You have no idea. Why do people meddle or make a big deal about nothing?"

He finishes his drink and sets his tumbler down. Strangely, he never turns to look at me, and for some reason, I find this mildly refreshing. This man wants to have a conversation and not try to pick me up or flirt. "For some, it's what they do; it's how they survive. For others, it's their way of caring."

"Well, the caring is a bit overboard in my opinion."

"What can I get you?" the bartender asks.

"Baileys please and whatever the gentleman is having." I motion toward the man who seems to speak with reason.

"Thank you," he says. "It's been years since a woman has bought me a drink. Usually, it's the man who offers."

"I didn't exactly offer. I suppose I should've asked if you wanted another."

This time he does turn, and when we make eye contact, he smiles. Except, there's something about him I find familiar, and it's not an oh-I'm-so-happy-to-see-you feeling. It's the stranger-danger-move-with-caution sense, which instantly makes me regret buying this man a drink. I take another look, wondering where it is I know him from. Certainly, not from around here and if he were friends of my parents, surely he'd go over and say something to my mother. I shake my head, trying to clear the cobwebs, to no avail. Still, something about him and the way he's speaking has the hairs on my neck standing at attention. Oddly enough, I haven't felt this way since I had a stalker, who is safely under observation elsewhere. The only thing I can deduce is that this man is paparazzi, making me thankful Calvin is with me... I try to smile, but it's forced, and I feel like he can sense this. Even as I turn away, I can feel his gaze still focused on me. I was stupid to suggest Calvin go with the guys tonight, but I wanted him to have fun and not resent me for ruining his vacation.

The bartender returns with my drink, and I pull it close to me, guarding it against errant hands that may come toward me. "Can you put this on my tab?" Surprisingly, my voice remains calm, even though the fight or flight senses are starting to kick in.

"You got it," he says.

"Well, enjoy your drink," I say to the man next to me, still being polite despite my need to run back to the safety of my group. He holds his glass up in salute as I slide off the stool. As quickly as I can, I rush back to the sofas we've been using for the evening.

"You look like you've seen a ghost," my mom says as I sit down with her and Eileen.

Shaking my head, I make an ill-fated attempt at grinning. "I don't know. There's something about that man at the bar. I get the impression I know him or at least have seen him, and our meeting wasn't favorable."

"Paparazzi?" Mindy asks.

"No, I don't think so. I mean, why would they come to Ramona Falls?"

Eileen pulls her phone out and aims in his direction. "What are you doing?" I pull her hand down before he can turn around.

"What?" She shrugs. "I can run him through facial recognition on the web and see if he comes up."

My mom gasps. Mindy claps. I roll my eyes. "You can't do that... or can you?" Now my interests are piqued.

Eileen grins like a cheshire cat. "Definitely. When my sister brought her boyfriend home, I snapped a picture of him and loaded it to see if he showed up in places he shouldn't."

"That's rather sneaky," Mom says. "But I like it."

"How do I not know this? You could totally revolutionize the dating game."

Mindy laughs so loud; others turn to see what's going on in our section. " I can see it now, '*Hollywood Starlet makes any potential suitor vying for her attention post personal photos before agreeing to a date.*'"

I toss the throw pillow in her direction but completely

116

miss her. "Laugh now, but think of the heartache it would save."

"You're, right D. You would've known Trey was an epic douche," Mindy says.

The cheerfulness I had been feeling quickly subsides until I play back the week prior. Mindy's right. If I had known, I would've never dated him. I suppose we all learn from our mistakes at some point in our lives. "Well, Trey is happily doing whatever..." I trail off, knowing our break-up was for the best.

SIXTEEN

"*D*elaney said we could use the suite she reserved or sit down along the ice," Dominic tells us as he walks ahead of us to enter the TD Garden.

"The suite could be fun," Gio says. "Watching the game from above is always an experience."

"But the ice is where all the action is. Especially if there's a brawl," I point out.

"What's going on here?" Calvin asks. He seems to tense up at the vast mass of people lingering around.

"This is North Station," I tell him.

"I thought we were going to hockey?"

"We are." I point to retractable glass walls where many Bruins and Canadiens fans are vying to head up the escalators once the walls push back. "The arena is upstairs."

"Say again?" Calvin looks at the three of us, clearly shocked by what I said.

"It's upstairs," Gio adds. "The Celtics and Bruins play above the station. The view is amazing."

Gio's right, if you're there to look at the view. Most of the time, it goes unnoticed though because people who come to the games are used to it. I like to take a look every now and again, be thankful I'm able to go to a game.

"People in New England are odd."

Gio, Dominic and I all laugh. Calvin isn't thinking anything we don't already about the folks on the "left" coast. We often have a tourist roll through town, wholly awed by our small town living. To us, it's all we know. To the visitors, we're living some idyllic dream, as if we've been plucked out of a magazine and set there for all the world to see.

The doors open and the mad rush to get upstairs starts. Gio holds us back for a few minutes to let the diehards go first. I've never understood why people hurry to get to their seats an hour early. I know for most it's to watch warm-ups, but the seats aren't the most comfortable, and personally, I'd rather wait.

"What's the plan?" Dom asks. "Seats or suite?"

"The seats are along the ice, right?" Gio asks and we all nod. Delaney spared no expense when she hooked us up with tickets. I had no idea about the suite until we were half way here. If I weren't feeling bad about seats to begin with, the suite definitely pushed me over the edge. I'm not trying to look a gift horse in the mouth, but I'm having a hard time accepting I can't return the favor to Delaney.

"Why not do both?" Calvin suggests. The four of us sort of look at each other like one of us has to make a decision. It's not going to be me, but I'll definitely go along with whatever is decided. I've never known what a luxury box has to offer, but I've heard stories.

"Can we?" Gio asks as we stand on the escalator. When we get to the top, he has all four tickets scanned. The lady smiles and directs us to the elevator we need to access the suite.

"Yeah, I've done it before. It's nice because we can eat

in the suite when the Bruins are attacking the other end of the ice," Dominic says as he motions us to follow him.

The suite's fully stocked by the time we get there. Delaney has clearly gone overboard and arranged for a vast selection of food to be ready and waiting for us to devour. There's everything from wings, to nachos, to pasta, not to mention a fully stocked soda bar, which has me laughing.

"What's so funny, Fisher?"

"Your sister made sure none of us are drinking on her tab." The look on Dom's face is priceless, and the snicker from Calvin causes me to laugh even harder. "Seriously, I could kiss her for this," I say, only to realize my choice of words. My mouth shuts quickly as my gaze falls to Gio. He's smiling, almost as if he didn't hear those words slip out. I immediately head over to the table of food and start making a plate. In the background, I can hear Dominic on the phone with Delaney, hopefully thanking her for everything and not whining because his favorite beverage isn't here.

"He takes advantage of his sister." Calvin picks up a plate and starts loading an assortment of food onto it. "I hear her on the phone with him a lot."

"Really? Like how?" I ask, only to shake my head. "You know what, it's none of my business."

"It's not mine either, but I have an opinion about siblings who aren't famous. They whine and ask for a lot without coming out and saying it."

"What do you mean?" I ask.

Calvin motions toward the other end of the room, away from where Dominic is. I glance around for Gio and find he's not here.

"He went to the restroom," Calvin says, knowing I was looking for Gio. "From my experience, siblings tend to go on and on about the same things until the famous one gives in.

The repetitiveness wears them down, and they finally act so the other will stop talking."

"You're very observant."

"It's my job and something I pride myself on. Being a police officer isn't any different, right? Our jobs aren't that different. I just spend more time with my employer."

"No, I suppose it's not, but sometimes I feel unfocused."

"Like when Delaney's name's brought up?"

My hand freezes on it's way to my mouth, which of course stays open until my brain decides to start functioning again and I close it. As casually as I can, I set my nacho filled chip down onto my plate and clear my throat. "Um... we used to be friends."

"And you're not now?"

I shrug. "I think as people grow up, the definition of friendship changes. I'm sure everyone wants to be her friend."

"They do, but her circle is very limited. You'd be surprised by her life."

"Oh, I've seen her in the papers," I tell him, thankful I've dodged his earlier statement.

Calvin adjusts his large frame in the leather chair. "The real Delaney is nothing like you see in the media. She prefers to stay home and watch movies, over going to a party or a club. When you see her, it's out of obligation. Either a director wants her someplace, or a company wants her dressed in their clothing, so they pay her to be in the right spot for a photo."

"Really?"

He nods and starts in on his plate of food, leaving me to my thoughts. For years, seeing Delaney in the news, I thought she enjoyed having her picture taken, the glitz and glam that comes with being a Hollywood star, and the all-night parties Heather often read about. She used to tell me the things she read about Delaney, the things she was doing and what was going on in her love life. I never knew it was all a ruse.

"My wife used to keep me updated on Delaney, and we'd go see her movies when they would come out."

"Used to?"

I nod and look at the ice where the teams are warming up. The arena is starting to fill up with people, and the noise level is getting louder. "She died almost two years ago, but up until she became sick, she was one of those people who bought every magazine and read it cover to cover. Of course, with Delaney being our local hero, everyone kept tabs on her."

"I think coming home was the right thing for her," he adds. I agree, mostly because I know her family is happy to have her home for the holidays. "You avoided my statement though."

"About what?" I ask, pretending I don't have a clue as to what he's talking about. Honestly, I feel like I'm in some warped version of reality television where the guys sit around and talk about their feelings, not the women. I think Calvin and I need to open a bottle of wine and light a few candles.

Calvin laughs. "It's okay. I get it. She's easy to crush on."

"I don't have a crush."

He nods. "If you say so."

I do say so. I don't have time for childhood crushes or any other flirtation game, especially when it comes to Delaney. It'd be pointless considering how different our lives are. I'm here, a full-time single dad raising an impressionable young daughter, and Delaney's everywhere, she doesn't need my baggage to slow her down. Not that I've considered being with her or even stand a chance at being someone in her life. I'm no different than everyone else in town. We're all star struck where she's concerned.

"So anyway, how long have you worked for Delaney?" I ask, steering the conversation in a different direction.

"A few years now. I came on after Delaney had a run in with a stalker."

"And your family is okay with you being here?"

"I'm not married. I'm also one of eight kids so if I'm not home for the holidays, my mother doesn't necessarily miss me. She has a dozen plus grandkids running around, taking up her attention."

"One of eight, huh? I thought I had a problem with my sister growing up, always in my stuff, bugging me every five seconds about whether one of my friends liked her. I can't imagine having seven of them."

Calvin laughs and nods toward Dominic. I turn to find him chatting with a few guys I don't know. "That's what I'm talking about. Our suite is private, and they shouldn't be in here. I should go find our seats before I say something Delaney won't like." He gets up and tosses his plate in the trash. I make the quick decision to follow him down. In the corridor, we run into Gio, who tells us he'll be down soon.

We find our seats quickly, and except for almost zero legroom, which affects Calvin more than it does me, but the seats are fantastic. "Do you like hockey?"

"I've only seen it on TV. I stick mostly to basketball and football. Delaney is nice enough to take me to the Laker games and bought season tickets to the Rams."

"You seem to be more than a bodyguard."

"Nope," he says matter-of-factly. "I'm just the guy who doesn't beg her for attention or disrespect her in the media."

His jab against the media gives me pause. I feel like I'm missing something, but I'm not sure what. I know I can look her up and see what's been going on in her life or even listen to the women who gossip like birds on a telephone wire, but I've prided myself on staying out of the Ramona Falls rumor mill as much as I can. Being a part of it when Delaney came back was enough to last me a good year or two. Besides, you never know who's telling the truth.

Dominic and Gio join us in time for the national anthem. Gio's excited and asks the arena photographer to take our photo. I'm sure for him, being away from his mayoral duties for the night is a reprieve.

Within seconds of the puck dropping, the Bruins score. A majority of the fans cheer, while the rest boo.

"Boston is a tough crowd," Calvin yells into my ear.

"It's the rivalry. If you have time, you should have Delaney take you to Montreal. The city is beautiful. It's a bit cold, but there's an underground walkthrough, which has shops and restaurants to check out. The Cathedral is a sight to behold during the holidays."

"She mentioned something about going iceskating at Rockefeller Center."

"Sounds like Delaney. She loves to skate."

"So I've been told. I think skating extends my guard duty into hazard pay. I believe there has to be some rule about a man my size being on blades."

I point to defenseman Zdeno Chára. "If he can do it, so can you, big guy."

Calvin gives me a side glare, making me laugh. I need this, though. I need to feel like I'm free from the stress, even if it's for a few hours.

SEVENTEEN

DELANEY

*T*he uneasy feeling I had the other night when I was with my mom, Mindy and Eileen hasn't gone away. I find myself looking over my shoulder even with Calvin by my side. I haven't told him about the encounter mostly because I feel like I could be overreacting. Maybe the man was harmless, and I misinterpreted the way he was gazing at me. I'm an actress; it's my job to be overdramatic at times.

If Calvin doesn't quit today, he will by the end of the month with all the random things I have planned. When I was growing up, I always worked the local tree stand, helping people find the right tree for them. At first, my job was to clean up and direct people, then it changed to taking payments and helping them carry trees to their car. I've always been too short to help anyone strap their tree down, but Dominic, Aiden or any one of their friends would be around to help.

Today, it's Calvin. As he stands there in the front of my rental, looking entirely out of place, I reach up on my tiptoes and pinch his cheek. He bats my hand away and glares at me. "This will be fun," I tell him.

"There's nothing fun about tree sap, pine needles, and cold weather," he bites back.

"True, but we have hot chocolate, candy canes, and Christmas music. Plus, in between customers you can hang out in the sugarhouse and get to know Mr. Steve. He's retired and spends his days tending to his garden, boiling sap to make maple syrup and growing Christmas trees. "

"And snow, wind and acres of trees. I'm not comfortable with you walking through with some unknown person, carrying a saw," he says.

"I'll be fine."

"Then why am I here?" Calvin has a point. I called him here because of the incident at the mall, and while nothing has happened per se, he's here because I feel safer when he's around. I nod, agreeing that traipsing through the uncut trees is probably not the best idea. Nor do I remember the lay of the land very well.

"I promise to stay right here." I turn and look at the rows of split rail fencing and saw horses used to hold the trees up.

"And no carrying any trees. The last thing you need is to get injured before you're due on set for your next film."

Internally, I groan. Being home has been incredibly relaxing to the point where I don't necessarily miss California, except for the weather. I know I have to go back, but the thought of staying here longer is very appealing or at least making sure I'm home in between movies. I could be a diva and demand a small break in between films. It's not likely I'd do something like that because I don't want to tarnish my reputation. However, the thought is there, lingering in the back of my mind.

Calvin and I walk down the snow-covered driveway

and into the sugarhouse where the wood stove is emitting a bit of warmth. "Mr. Steve!" I don't give the old man a chance to recognize me before I'm tugging him into an embrace. "How have you been?"

He pulls back and appraises me. I give him my best dazzling smile, praying he remembers me. Maybe this was a mistake. I never thought he'd forget about me, but ten years have passed, and when my dad mentioned volunteering, I jumped at the opportunity.

"Well, well, well, if it isn't little Du Luca. I see your ole man is making you earn your keep."

"He's a slave driver, I tell ya." Mr. Steve hugs me again before extending his hand out to Calvin. "Mr. Steve, this is my friend, Calvin Johnson."

"So you're the bodyguard I've heard rumblings about around town?"

"Guilty as charged," Calvin says. "And here to be of service to you."

"Well, I appreciate the help. The kids these days, it's hard to find someone willing to be out in the cold for hours on end. They always want to play on their phones or sit in front of the television where it's warm."

"I have to say, I agree with them. It's cold here, Mr. Steve." Calvin solidifies his comment by crossing his arms and shivering. I know he can't be that cold since he's wearing a state-of-the-art-nothing-is-getting-through-parka. In fact, I'm wearing the same type, and I'm toasty warm.

"I'll keep the fire roaring, the drinks flowing and the college games on the television."

"Sounds good," Calvin says just as a car pulls in. I rush outside to greet my first customers in over ten years.

Today's going to be a challenge, I know this, but am secretly hoping word spreads that I'm here and business is booming. Some would frown on me for having an ulterior motive other than volunteering. I'm okay with that. I want people to flock to the tree farm, to buy local and to have fun. If I have to use my star power to make it happen, I'm going to do it.

The morning starts slowly, but by the afternoon business is picking up. My dad and Dominic are here to help people with their tree selection, and to lend a hand cutting and stocking new trees.

"Couldn't stay away, huh?"

I turn at the sound of a familiar voice and lay my eyes on Aiden and his daughter. Holly gives me a small wave, which I happily return. "I couldn't. I love this place."

"Really? Because I remember someone complaining about getting sap in her hair, breaking her fingernails and smelling like trees back in the day."

I look away sheepishly. "Sometimes it takes not having something like this to make you realize how much you miss it."

Aiden leans down and whispers something into Holly's ear. It seems like his blue eyes never leave mine nor does the smile change on his face.

"I know, Daddy. I already met her," Holly whispers loudly. Aiden looks surprised by Holly's admission. I rack my brain, trying to remember if I told him about my involvement with the school play.

"I told you, right, because I feel like I did the other day when we were having breakfast."

He straightens up and ever so slowly, a grin appears. "Are you serious right now? Making me question my sanity on whether or not we've had this conversation? You're lucky there isn't a snowball in my hand right now."

Holly giggles, and it's the best sound in the world. "I hit Daddy with a snowball the other night."

"You did?"

She nods eagerly. "Yep, we attacked him."

"Well, I think this is the most amazing news I've heard in a long time." I smirk at Aiden, who rolls his eyes.

"It was so funny. Daddy had snow everywhere."

I squat down until I'm Holly's height, which honestly doesn't take much. I reach for her mitten-clad hand and hold it in mine. "What do you say we go look for your tree and we can talk about how I'm going to seek revenge on your father for making me feel silly?"

"Daddy, may I?" Holly looks up at Aiden, seeking permission. I want to applaud her for not going with me. I'm not so sure I would've done the same if my idol were crouched before me, offering to take me someplace.

"Do you mind if I come with you ladies?"

Holly turns to me, and I shrug. "Fine with us," she says to her father. Still, I don't let go of Holly's hand when we start the tour, up and down the rows of trees.

"What kind of tree are you looking for?" I make it a point to ask her.

"I want a big fluffy one that's really, really tall."

I look to Aiden for confirmation, but he's shaking his head. I direct us toward the row where the narrower and shorter trees are, pulling out the first one I see. "How about this one? I named him Arnie."

"You named the tree?" Aiden questions me.

"I did. I named every tree out here today. It gives them a sense of personality, provides him or her with the hope that they'll be adopted."

"Adopted? It's a tree, Laney."

"Not just any tree, Fish, but a *Christmas* tree. It's going to bring hope, cheer and a lasting impression for years to come."

"Daddy, why does she call you Fish?"

Aiden and I laugh. I don't recall when it started, but it was sometime before we started dating. Of course, boys call all their friends by their last name, and I wanted to be different. He, in turn, called me Laney and he's the only one ever to do so.

"It's a nickname, just like I call you Punky." Holly smiles at her dad, making it easy to see how much she loves him. He kneels down and wraps his arm around her waist. "What do you think, Punky? Do you want to take Arnie home?"

Holly gives the tree a once over before shaking her head. "He's missing some branches, and I *really* want a girl tree. Can we please have a girl tree, Daddy?"

"Do you have any girl trees?" Aiden asks.

"Sure do, right over here." The Fishers follow me to another rack where I contemplate which tree to show them. I finally set one up right and introduce them to Gwen. "She was cut this morning."

"I love Gwen," Holly says, clapping her hands. The muffled sound is loud enough for me to hear. I start cheering right along the side of her.

"Where will Gwen live in your house?" I ask as I prepare to carry the tree back to the sugarhouse, only to have Aiden stop me in my tracks.

"I got this," he says as his hand brushes against mine. Gloves or not, I felt something spark between us. My hand stays under his until Holly's voice breaks the spell.

"... the big window and she'll have lights and pretty ornaments. We have an angel to go up top."

"This sounds amazing, Holly. Maybe I'll be able to see Gwen when she's all decorated."

"Oh yes. Daddy, can Delaney come over? I can show her my room, and maybe we can watch a movie together." Holly looks at Aiden with the most serious expression on her face. I do the same, giving Aiden a stare down, waiting for him to provide us with an answer.

"Well, I'm sure Delaney is busy."

Not exactly the answer I was looking for, but he's right. I'm busy. With what, I don't exactly know, aside from making and eating every cookie that comes out of the oven.

Aiden settles his tab while Calvin puts Gwen into the back of Aiden's truck. Holly and I look at the wreaths Mr. Steve's wife has made, and I tell her to pick one. She does and hands it to Calvin, who sets it into the truck.

Aiden gets Holly situated, and comes over to me. "Thank you for this."

"I didn't do anything, Fish."

"No, you did. I didn't mean to forget about our conversation the other day; it's just... seeing you here brought up a few memories, and they caught me off guard. I wanted to thank you for the other night. Hanging out with your dad, Dom and Calvin was a lot of fun."

"Calvin said you guys had a good time."

"We did, but what you did here, with naming the trees and entertaining Holly like that... well let me say this, you took something as mundane as picking out a tree and made it into a production. You're so good at what you do. You have no idea the effect you have on her. I appreciate this."

"Fish..." I want to tell him I wasn't acting, and that I enjoyed every second I spent with him and his daughter, but he doesn't give me a chance.

He shakes his head and turns toward his truck, leaving me standing there with my mouth open and my thoughts running a mile a minute. My mom and Mindy have both said things have been hard for him. Maybe there's something I can do to help or bring some cheer to his and Holly's lives.

EIGHTEEN

AIDEN

*T*he constant chatter about how amazing, cool, super neat and so pretty Delaney is, filled the silent void on the way back to our house. Even if I wanted, I couldn't find a single point to disagree on with Holly. However, I did want to elaborate on a few, such as how incredible she is. In seconds, she turned what could've easily been a boring outing into a fun-laugh filled adventure, making my daughter giggle and smile so brightly that I found myself feeling happy for the first time in a while.

This type of happy is different from what I felt when I was at the hockey game or when there are a few extra dollars in my paycheck. This was one of those moments you don't forget, and pray can be emulated next year and the year after so it gives you and your child something to talk about and remember as the years go by. Without knowing it, Delaney changed the scope of Holly's Christmas.

"Look at all the lights," Holly says, staring out the window at the houses we pass by. There was a time when Heather and I joked about going all Griswold with decorating. Luckily, we came to our senses and went with a more simplistic and understated feel, stringing up white lights along the eaves of the roof and wrapping the shrubs and the base of the large tree in our front yard. "Which house do you like best, Daddy?"

Slowing down, I look out the windows, shocked by how many people have their holiday lights on and it's barely dusk. The houses near our street are nice, but nothing like what the Du Lucas and their neighbors do. Growing up, everyone flocked to Dominic and Delaney's street. Not only for their Christmas displays but Halloween as well. I'm tempted to drive Holly over and show her, but it'll have to wait.

"I think next week, I'll take you somewhere to show you all my favorite decorations," I tell her. "There's a place in town where every house decorates. They play music, and on the weekends, some of the owners will have cookies and hot cocoa for people."

"Really?" Holly's voice has a level of excitement that I haven't heard in a long time.

"Really," I say back to her, matching her enthusiasm. I stop driving so I can glance at my daughter. She's oblivious to the struggles I face daily. It's the way it should be.

"Can we make cocoa when we get home?"

"Yeah, I think tonight definitely calls for some hot chocolate."

"With marshmallows?" She looks at me excitedly.

I press the gas pedal to continue our drive home. "What would hot cocoa be at Christmastime without marshmallows? I think tonight calls for the whole bag." Holly starts clapping, and from my peripheral, I can see her squiggling in her seat. Normally, I limit the amount she can have.

Our house is dark when we pull into the driveway. After I turn off the truck, I find myself staring at it, praying for some Christmas miracle to come along and miraculously fix everything that's wrong with it. The list of repairs and upgrades is long. The only thing I can do is tackle the smaller projects one at a time.

The opening of Holly's door shakes me from my dream-like state. I follow quickly, running ahead to turn the lights on for her. As usual, the house is cold, and I don't hesitate to crank the heat. She turns on the radio and twists the dial, increasing the volume of the Christmas song playing. I cringe, but let it go. She needs this, and honestly, I do too.

Holly and I work as a team to bring our decorations up from the basement. With all our boxes piled up in the living room, I head back out to bring our tree in. Thankfully, it hasn't snowed in the past few days, so the tree is relatively dry.

"Have you seen the tree stand?" I ask, propping the tree against the kitchen wall.

"Right here, but it has a hole in it."

Holly brings the stand over, and sure enough, the bottom has rusted out. This is one of those learning moments. Heather told me to buy a plastic one a few years back, but I never got around to doing it.

"What are we going to do?" Holly asks.

The thing is, I don't know. The hardware store is already closed, and the nearest store is a bit of a drive. Leaving now means we won't get to decorate until tomorrow evening. Not necessarily a bad thing except I already promised Holly a night of fun.

"What if Mr. Steve has one?" Holly suggests but does so in a way that makes me laugh because she's shrugged her shoulders and put her hands up, almost as if she's not sure her idea is worthy or somehow telling me I should've thought of this first.

"I'll call him and see." I pull my phone out, scroll through my contacts and press his number. "Steve's Tree Farm."

"Dom?"

"What's up?"

"Hey, man, this is Aiden. Does Mr. Steve sell tree stands?"

"Let me check." Dominic covers the phone and hollers out. There's mumbling in the background, but I can't make heads or tails of what's being said. "Nah, but he's sending my dad over with one. Says you can return it after the holidays."

I give Holly the thumbs up, which results in her jumping up and down. "Great. Please tell him, and your dad thank you."

"Will do." Dom hangs up but not before I hear Delaney laugh. Part of me wonders what made her laugh, while the other part of me wishes I were there to witness it.

While I heat up the milk for our festive drinks, Holly starts opening the boxes. I've decided I'm not going to dictate where she puts things. I want her imagination to run wild and be free when it comes to decorating. I think it'll mean more to her. I know it will to me.

With the music on and our mugs full, I take on the dubious task of straightening out the strings of lights. I don't care how nicely wrapped I made them last year, somehow they've all become a tangled mess. This right here, makes me want to get a fake tree, but I can't do that to Mr. Steve.

Lights shine through our front window, alerting us to Gio's arrival. "The mayor is here," I tell Holly. "I'm going to go out and meet him." I may have known the Du Lucas for most of my life, but inviting Gio into my home is something I'm not comfortable with.

She runs to the window to look. "That's not the mayor."

"Oh?" I to look out the window, only to find Delaney walking past my truck with a tree stand in her hand, disappearing into my dooryard. Holly's screeching has me rushing to the door. Holly opens it before I can stop her and meet Delaney outside. I'm a step or two behind when Holly invites Delaney in. To Holly, having a movie star in your house is probably a huge moment in your life. To me, it's anxiety overload.

Our eyes meet, and the smile she gives me has me forgetting for a moment that we're standing in my kitchen. "Mr. Steve wanted me to bring this over." Delaney hands me the plastic tree base.

"I thought your dad—"

"I wanted to," she says, interrupting me.

"Do you want to stay and help us decorate?"

"Oh, no—" I start to say, only to hear Delaney blurt out, "I'd love to."

In the blink of an eye, Holly is pulling Delaney into our living room and offering her my mug of hot chocolate. I should feel dejected, but seeing Holly's excitement changes everything.

"Do you want me to hold Gwen so you can put her on the base?"

I look down at the contraption in my hand and nod. Even if I wanted to ask Delaney to leave, upsetting Holly isn't worth it. I have to suck up my pride and give my daughter this.

Delaney holds Gwen upright, lifting when I tell her to, so I can make sure the trunk is secure. Holly tells us she'll get the water for Gwen. "You don't have to stay," I tell Delaney. "I'm sure you're busy. Holly will understand."

She shrugs. "I have nowhere else I'd rather be." I want

to believe that's true, but I'm sure the list of places she should be is rather long.

"Where's Calvin?"

"Sitting in the sugarhouse, at least he was when I left."

"And you don't need to be with him?"

Delaney chuckles. "Something tells me you and Holly aren't going to corner me and demand my autograph or shove a camera in my face."

"Holly might. She's a fan and known to be vicious." I wink.

Holly returns, walking slowly with two large cups of water. When I try to help her, she tells me she can do it herself. The whole time, she's talking to the tree, as if it's her best friend.

"Can I offer you something to drink?"

"We have hot cocoa with marshmallows. Daddy can make you one while we start decorating," Holly tells Delaney.

"Perfect!" Delaney raises an eyebrow and smirks. Yep, I've become the errand boy while my daughter monopolizes the starlet's time. It's okay; I know my place.

For the time it took me to make Delaney's drink, the ladies placed lighted garland on the mantel and plug it in as I enter the living room. "Wow, I never thought to put it there before." I hand Delaney the mug and stand back, watching as Holly holds Heather's stocking in her hand. I wait to see what she's going to do, letting her decide on whether it'll go up or not. She sets it aside, pulls her own out of the box, and places it on the snowman hook. Mine follows right after.

I don't say anything.

I just watch.

Delaney must sense the shift in my demeanor because

she proclaims that the music isn't loud enough and that Gwen is naked and in need of some lights. "Chop, chop," she says.

"Yeah, Daddy. Gwen is nakie!" Holly giggles and runs to one of the boxes and pulls out the angel. I go to her and lift her up, while Delaney helps Holly place it on top. "She's beautiful."

"She will be once I get the lights on and Gwen is decorated." I set Holly down and get to work on the lights. Delaney helps every step of the way. Once the lights are on, her and Holly start placing the ornaments on the tree. While they focus their attention there, I set all our other decorations out. Within the hour, the house is warm, festive and full of laughter.

"Okay, I think we're ready," Delaney says.

I shut off all the lights and press the switch that will turn on the white lights, to illuminate Gwen.

"Ah, she's so pretty," Holly proclaims excitedly.

"Wow. You both did an amazing job."

"Of course we did, Daddy."

I look at Delaney, who hasn't taken her eyes off the tree. "What do you think?"

She looks over and smiles. We maintain eye contact for longer than what should be socially acceptable. "I think it's one of the most beautiful trees I've ever seen." Her statement gives me pause. Surely, her mother's tree or any one of the fancy trees she encounters in Los Angeles are prettier than the one she's standing in front of, I would have thought.

"It's snowing! It's snowing! Daddy, can we go out?" Holly tugs on my shirt, causing me to look away from Delaney. I glance out the window, and sure enough, it's coming down in sheets, the wind is blowing, and I can barely see the outline of Delaney's car.

"I don't remember hearing about a snowstorm tonight."

"Me neither," Delaney adds. "I hope my car is still out there."

"Do you think Frosty took it?" Holly asks, and just like that, the mood shifts from the possible gloom to cheerful.

Delaney gasps. "How will I ever get home?"

Holly shrugs. "You can just sleep over."

I deadpan and sneak a glance at Delaney, whose eyes are wide, yet she's grinning from ear to ear. I'm at a loss, not sure what I should say. I open my mouth, but words fail me.

"Come on I have jammies you can wear." Holly takes Delaney's hand and pulls her behind me. If Delaney is pleading for help, she doesn't show it. I don't know what to do. Do I follow? Do I stay here? Do I hurry down to my bedroom and change my sheets?

"Please someone tell me what to do," I mutter to myself seconds before the power goes out.

NINETEEN

DELANEY

There's a loud bang. Holly gasps and starts to jump into my arms, only to have the power go out. We smack heads, both of us crying out in pain. She lets out a soft whimper, and automatically my embrace tightens around her. "Are you okay?"

"Uh huh. I'm scared."

"It'll be okay. I'm sure your dad can fix it." That's what dads do; they fix everything. I stand, and Holly's legs go around my waist. She's not letting go of me, even if I wanted to put her down. I shuffle my feet toward her door, hoping I can get there without stepping on anything. She's seven, and the clutter in her room reflects that.

When I heard Aiden needed a tree stand I didn't hesitate to bring it over. I want to feel useful while I'm here, and honestly I'm a bit tired of everyone handling me with kid gloves. My mom won't let me cook or use the oven, out of fear I'll burn myself, which is ridiculous. She's worried I'll do something to mess up my next movie role. Calvin refuses to let me drive, which I get. It's his job to be by my side and protect me. Dominic... well, he doesn't care what I do, as long as he benefits from it somehow. Yes, it seems rude, but I made a promise to him when we were younger that he'd get to relish in the perks of my success, and he hasn't let me forget it. My dad, on the other hand, had no qualms tossing me his keys. Of course, the look he gave me threw me off kilter a bit. Instead of staying and asking him why he was making funny eyes at me, I hightailed it out of Mr. Steve's with the tree stand in my hand.

I intended to drop the stand off and head home, at least that's what I kept saying to myself as I drove over here. When Holly invited me in and asked me to stay, I couldn't say no. Maybe I should've, but there's something between Aiden and me that I feel is worth exploring. I'm not looking for a relationship, and according to every woman in town, neither is he, but I'd like to re-establish the friendship we once had. I know I'm to blame for the lack of communication. I didn't stay in touch with anyone, but being back here now, I want everything to be different. I'm going to make the necessary changes to keep Ramona Falls a part of my life.

Much like Holly's bedroom, the hallway is pitch black. The noise down the hall has my heart beating a bit faster than normal, and the howling wind can be heard through the walls. Holly's grip tightens with each step I take toward the living room. I don't know why, but I'm treating this like a scene from a movie. Although, I've never done any horror movies and if I have to feel like this — uneasy and unsure, I'd rather stick to rom-coms and romance.

"Fish?" I call out and receive no response.

"Where's Daddy?"

"Probably outside." I finally make it into the living room where the large picture window does give off a bit of light from the moon reflecting on the snow. Holly and I sit on the couch and wrap up with the afghan that's draped over the back.

"My mommy made this," she says, putting the blanket up to her chin.

"It's beautiful."

If the power weren't out, sitting here would be peaceful with the heavily falling snow, even though it's impossible for me to get home. The morning after a storm is my favorite time. There's nothing better than driving down a tree-lined road, under a canopy of snow with the sun shining bright against the snow. Storms like this are a photographer's dream. They'll be able to capture nature at her best once the sun rises.

The kitchen door flies open, startling Holly and I. I set her aside so I can close the door, only for Aiden to walk in with his arms full of wood. "Let me help you."

"Can you shut the door?"

"Of course."

Aiden dumps the pile of wood into the box by the fireplace and drops down to his knees. "I bet you ladies are cold."

"We are, Daddy."

He looks over his shoulder, toward Holly and pauses. "Do you need me to do anything?" I ask.

"Can you make sure her coat is ready? I haven't used this fireplace for a few years, and I'm not sure what kind of draft we're going to get."

"Yes, of course. Do you have a flashlight, Fish?"

"Cupboard next to the refrigerator."

Right. Got it. Except I don't, and I'm trying not to panic. I fumble through the kitchen, barely escaping a toe-stubbing accident and use my hands to guide my way until I've reached the cool metal of the flashlight. I press the button, and it comes on instantly. "So much better," I say with relief.

I do as Aiden asks, making sure all of Holly's stuff is ready to go in the event we have to evacuate. It's only when I pick up my coat, does my cell fall out of my pocket. I bring it to life; surprised I still have cell service here. It's always been questionable here.

Numerous texts are sitting there, unread. Most of them are from Calvin, asking if he needs to come pick me up. The last thing I want is for him or anyone else to drive in this storm, and honestly, I don't want to leave Aiden and Holly.

There's a soft glow coming from the fireplace, illuminating Aiden. His back is to me, giving me the perfect opportunity to stare at him. Under his bulky clothes I imagine his muscles are straining each time he stokes the fire and how much he must feel a sense of pride for making sure his little girl has heat.

My phone vibrates again with a text from Calvin. I open it and reply with: I'm fine. See you in the morning, before shutting it off. The weather turned what could've been a quick night into the slumber party Holly wants to have.

"The fire feels great," I say, standing next to Aiden with my hands hovering toward the opening.

"Thanks. As I said, I don't normally use it."

"Why not? It's a great source of heat."

Aiden shakes his head slightly and doesn't answer. I use this as my cue to go back to Holly. She's lying down, watching her father as he builds a fire, but as soon as I sit, she crawls into my lap and nestles into me.

"What's it like to make a movie?" she asks.

"Oh boy... well, it can be a lot of fun, but can also be a lot of work. I have to memorize my lines and say them repeatedly, all while someone is telling me what to do. However, I get to play dress up all the time, and someone is always playing with my hair and doing my makeup."

"That sounds fun."

"It can be." My fingers start moving through her hair. She looks up and smiles.

"What else?" Aiden asks. He sits down in the middle of the couch, his leg touching mine. I make zero effort to move.

"Well, let's see. Sometimes I get to travel and go to these amazing places to shoot the movies. Other times, they're done on a studio lot."

"What's that?" Holly asks.

"It's a giant place where a lot of television shows are filmed, along with commercials, movies, and a few other things. Someday, I'll show you."

"You will?" she asks, sitting up straighter. "You mean I can come to your house?"

"Of course, you and your dad can come anytime you want."

I can feel Aiden's eyes on me. I'm hesitant to look at him, knowing I've overstepped. It happens. I get excited. I haven't been able to be me in a long time. I mean sure, Holly's asking about making movies, but somehow her questions feel different. She's not doing it to be intrusive. She wants to know about me and my life.

"Tell me, are you a Girl Scout?"

She nods, and a yawn quickly follows. "A Brownie. I'm earning my badges."

"I was a Brownie too when I was your age. I couldn't wait to become a Girl Scout so I could sell cookies."

"Cookies are my favor..." another yawn cuts off her words.

"Why don't I take you to bed, Holly." Aiden reaches for

his daughter. Only she snuggles deep into the hole between my body and the back of the couch.

"No, I want to stay with Delaney, and I don't have a nightlight."

"It's late," he states.

"I'll go to sleep right here." Holly closes her eyes, causing Aiden and me to chuckle. He shakes his head, clearly admitting defeat. When he doesn't reach for her, I adjust slightly, giving her more space, and making sure she's covered.

There's a long bit of silence, where only the crackling of the fire, the whistling wind, and our breathing fills the void.

"How's work?" I ask, breaking the silence.

"I'm wondering if we should announce our intent to marry tomorrow while I'm at church or wait until the tree lighting ceremony."

I can't hold back my laughter, even though I'm trying. Aiden and I both look at Holly, fearful that I might wake her. For a kid who closed her eyes to pretend to sleep, it didn't take her long to pass out. "I can call Calvin and ask him to come get me."

He shakes his head. "No, it's not worth it. No one should be driving in this stuff. I'll find a way to deal with your brother."

"He's as bad as my mother."

"He did learn from her," Aiden points out. "After the incident at the mall, he serenaded me with the hero song."

"No, he didn't?"

Aiden doesn't even have to confirm what he told me. I know Dominic well enough to know he'd do something ridiculous like that. "I'm sorry. He's just..."

"Dominic—"

"The donkey." I interrupt Aiden to finish. "I should ask

my parents if that's why they named him Dominic. Maybe they had a premonition before he was born."

Aiden does everything he can to hold back his laughter. Holly stirs, causing us both to cover our mouths. "No more jokes." He begs.

"I can't help it. Dom tortured me while I was growing up. I can at least poke fun at his name, especially at Christmastime. I think tomorrow I'm going to play it loudly and make snorting sounds when he comes home."

Aiden's eyes go wide. "Please, invite me over. This is something I have to see."

"Deal."

Aiden gets up to stir the fire, and I use the chance to readjust Holly, so I'm a little more comfortable. He takes the spot next to me, sitting so close our bodies are touching. He smells like wood, fire, and Christmas, all wrapped up. I'm tempted to inhale deeply, but don't want to come off as a weirdo. Instead, on the inside, I'm giddy as a schoolgirl sitting next to her crush.

"What's your one regret?" I ask him.

He takes a deep breath in and exhales slowly. "I don't know if I have any. I think that once you have a child, anything you wish you had done differently goes out the window because of the love you feel for them. What about you?"

"I would've told Dom to leave us alone."

"Laney..."

"No, just listen, Fish. For a long time, I always wondered if I missed my opportunity at my happily ever after. Hollywood is rough on life, love, and happiness, but I always thought I'd keep the small town girl with me even out there, and find my one and only. But it wasn't until you pulled me over that day and I looked into your eyes that I finally felt like I was home again. I know neither of us is in any place to be more than friends, but I do wonder if I had made different choices, how life would've been."

Aiden doesn't respond with words but does with the most fantastic gesture possible. He clasps his hand with mine and leans into me.

TWENTY

"What the..." My heart begins to beat rapidly as I look around. Every light is on and someone is going on about Santa bringing them a gift for Christmas. It takes me a minute to recognize the voice is coming from the radio. I'm also sweating and feel like I'm being trapped by something. That something is Delaney. She's resting against my side with her arm draped over my stomach, sleeping soundly despite the lights and noise. I suppose, in her line of work, you learn to sleep through anything.

Rubbing my hand over my face, I tap Delaney on her shoulder, trying to rouse her. I don't know what time we fell asleep or how she ended up next to me, but she is. Her lips purse into a little pout and her eyes flutter. I wonder if she's dreaming about being home in California or if Ramona Falls is invading her subconscious. Laney hasn't been home long but she's already had an impact on everyone around her. When she leaves to go back, people here will be torn. Holly will be devastated. After all, she's already attached to Delaney.

Holly isn't the only one.

Speaking of my daughter, she's at the end of the couch, with her legs resting on Delaney's. By the look of us, you'd wonder how any of us slept at all. I reach out and touch Holly's toes, but she doesn't budge either. We're a heaping pile of arms, legs and torsos on a couch meant for sitting, At a push, one person could sleep here, but it wouldn't be comfortable. I should know since my back is screaming in pain and my neck has a kink in it. I'm afraid to move out of fear I might pull a muscle.

Delaney mumbles incoherently but doesn't stir. It would be so easy to close my eyes and fall asleep with her but there's no way I can, not with the power back on. Carefully, I slide out from under her. The burning embers left over from the fire are still red and glowing. Using the poker, I spread them out, hoping to extinguish them before it's time to leave for church. Although, missing today might be a good idea. It's only going to take a matter of minutes for word to spread that Delaney spent the night. I wish her being here wasn't such a big deal to people, but small town lives need gossip to survive.

The plow truck thunders by, causing the front window to rattle. "Some day," I mutter, knowing the day will come when I can fix up this place.

"Some day, what?" Delaney asks from behind me. I look at her from over my shoulder. Her hair is a mess, matted to her face, and she has raccoon eyes.

"Some day, we're going to look back on this moment and realize—"

"Realize what?" she asks, stepping forward. Her hand rest on my forearm and the feel of her skin on mine causes a tingling sensation I haven't felt in years. Not since I first met Heather, and definitely not since Delaney and I dated. As coyly as possible, I drop my arm, not wanting to send the wrong message to Delaney. I like her, but we're too different.

"You're going to realize you let your guard down and your number one fan is going to see what you look like in the morning." I raise my eyebrows and try to smile while holding back a laugh. Her eyes go wide and she covers her face before letting out a groan. "Bathroom is first door on the right."

Delaney goes running; however it strikes me as odd she hadn't asked where it was before. I could say we were caught up in the moment, but I don't think that's the case. I cover the embers as much as I can before heading into the kitchen to make coffee. Looking through the window as I fill the pot, the snow glistens off the rising sun. This is when I love the covered ground. It's pristine and looks like a million crystals have fallen from the sky. Of course, out front will look gray and dirty by the end of the morning once cars are on the road, and yards becomes a trampled ice rink after everyone heads out to play and to build snowmen, igloos and battle walls for their snowball fights.

"I can't believe... hey, what're you doing?" I jump at the sound of Delany's voice and shut the water off, having to pour out the overflow.

"I spaced out." Setting the coffee pot down, I reach for a towel, only to have Delaney take over the coffee making. "I can do that," I tell her, but it's too late. She's already scooping coffee grounds into a fresh liner.

"You need a Keurig."

I nod. "I need a lot of things, but a fancy one cup coffee maker isn't one of them."

"Well maybe Santa will bring you one," she says, resting her hip against the counter. Looking at her, seeing her without her normal make-up, she looks nothing like the woman you see on the screen. Delaney's eyes somehow shimmer under the dull lighting in my kitchen. The pull I feel is magnetic, and I find myself stepping closer to her. My brain is screaming, telling me to stop, to step back and face reality. The reality being she doesn't live here. She'll be leaving eventually. We're not in the same league. My heart and my body control every action, every feeling right down to my pounding heart, sweaty palms and parched mouth.

My hand reaches out and cups her cheek. Her eyes close and her head tilts upward. I lick my lips in anticipation, leaving my mouth open for what surely will be a life-changing kiss. My eyes drift shut and the small gasp I hear from her pushes me forward. The air we breathe is the same, it's shared, and for the first time since my wife passed, I want to kiss another woman. I want to love her, cherish her and find every possible excuse to be with her, and yet I haven't even kissed her yet.

"Daddy?"

I jerk away from Delaney and she turns toward the coffee pot. I shake away the fairytale daydream I was having and go back to the living room where Holly is. Her hair, although blonde, matches the same state Delaney's was in not moments ago.

Clearing my throat and my thoughts, I push Holly's hair out of her face and look into her blue eyes. "Good morning. It's still early, do you want to go back to bed?"

She shakes her head. "Where's Laney?" she asks, tiredly. I want to correct her and tell her I'm the only one allowed to refer to Delaney that way, but I don't. It's not my place.

"I'm here, but I'm about to leave. I need to head home."

"But what about church?" Holly asks her.

Delaney and I make eye contact, but I can only hold it for a second. Delaney goes to Holly and pulls her into a hug. "I'll have to see what Calvin wants to do. I sort of left him with my brother yesterday."

"Daddy says Dominic is a royal pain—"

I cut Holly off before she can repeat what I've said about Dom, although it's nothing Delaney doesn't already know. "Okay, say goodbye to Delaney and tell her you'll see her..."

"At school," Delaney says.

"Okay," Holly whines. Believe me, kid. I get it.

"Holly, go change your clothes. I'm going to go clean off Delaney's car for her."

"Oh, I can do it." Delaney's hand touches my forearm and the sensation I felt earlier is back, but more powerful. The urge to pull her into my arms and to kiss her senseless is pressing.

"Don't be silly," I tell her. "I'll take care of it for you."

"That means you can help me get dressed!" Holly wastes no time reaching for Delaney's hand and tugs her down the hall. I half expect Delaney to look at me from over her shoulder and plead for help, but she doesn't, and I like that even though I shouldn't. But she does yell, "Keys are in my coat," as she continues down the hall. What happened or was about to happen in the kitchen should've never even come close. Kissing complicates friendships, and right now that's the only thing we can be.

By the time Delaney emerges from the house, her car is warming up, it's clear of snow and I'm about done blowing the snow from the driveway. She takes one look and starts laughing uncontrollably. "What's wrong?" I ask, shutting off the machine.

"You're covered in snow. If I didn't know better, I'd think you're a yeti."

I glance down at myself and nod. "I suppose I could've left the two feet of snow here and watched you back out." I raise my eyebrows, challenging her.

"You wouldn't do that." Delaney steps closer, placing her hands on the side of my snow covered jacket. Her head tilts back, leaving the pathway to her lips wide open. Kissing her will lead to heartache, and apparently, something my body doesn't care about because I'm moving closer.

"Hi, Mr. Fisher." Delaney turns away quickly. I step in front of her, blocking her from whoever is at the end of my driveway. From here, I can't make out their face, but that doesn't stop me from waving. "Will we see you at church?"

"Sure will," I say to the woman I'm assuming is my neighbor. I wait until she's past the snow bank, wondering what she's doing out this early and walking the streets.

"I should go," Delaney says as she opens the car door. Turning around, I grip the door, holding it open for her. I'm tempted to ask her if she's okay, but we both know what's coming. Whether my neighbor saw it was Delaney I was about to kiss or not, rumors will be rampant this morning because some mystery woman spent the night at my house.

"I'll see you later?" My statement comes out more like a question. I know I'll see her, I guess I want to know when.

"At church," she tells me, pulling the door shut and switching her car into reverse. I wait until she's on the road before I head back into the house. My discarded snowsuit hangs in the mudroom where it can dry before I have to put it on again. Inside, Holly is sitting at the table, finishing a bowl of cereal.

"Good girl, making your breakfast."

"I didn't," she says with a shrug. "Laney did."

"Did she do your hair as well?"

Holly turns to show me the French braid, which starts on one side of her head and finishes on the other. It's not a good feeling, knowing I'll never be able to do something like that for her. Maybe, what I'm feeling is a sign I'm ready to move on, that Holly needs a mother. Someone who can do her hair, teach her how to put her make-up on and tell girly secrets to.

While Holly continues eating breakfast, I shower and get dressed quickly. The benefit to having short hair is I don't have to do anything with it. The downfall, my head freezes in the winter and I need to wear a stocking cap or toque every time I have to leave the house. Brain freeze is a real thing and doesn't just happen when you eat ice cream too fast.

The church parking lot is full when we pull in. In fact, I can't remember a time when there's been so many cars. I help Holly out of the truck and when she sees my parents, she goes running. My sister stalks toward me with an angry scowl on her face. As soon as I see her hand rear back, I know she's going to hit me. I'm prepared though and step out of the way.

"I can't believe you."

"What?" I ask her, completely unaware of what her problem is.

"Shelby. You've broken her heart. I thought you were a better man than this, Aiden."

Shelby? Did I make plans with her and forget? I don't think I did, but I could be wrong. "It started snowing. I'll make it up to her."

"What?" Meredith asks.

"What, what?"

"You seriously have no idea what I'm talking about, do

you?" She crosses her arms over her chest and huffs. I shake my head slowly, unwilling to open my mouth out of fear I'll say something wrong. Meredith's hands flail about and she groans. "You spent the night with Delaney Du Luca. Everyone knows about it. People saw you making out this morning. Shelby is heartbroken, Aiden. She really likes you."

I hold my hands up. "First of all, Delaney spent the night because it started snowing and we had a power outage. She brought a tree stand over from Mr. Steve's and ended up helping Holly and I decorate. Second, Delaney and I weren't making out. Third, what I do in my home is my business and fourth, I never led Shelby to believe we were any more than friends."

"Hey, Aiden." The voice of Shelby has me looking over my sister's shoulder.

"Hi, Shelby."

"I want to know if I can count on you to help set up the park for the festival?" It's the way she says "count on you" that has me feeling guilty. Every year since I can remember, I've always helped out with the festival. Not that she'd know this since it's her first year taking over. I glimpse quickly at my sister, who's scowling at me.

"Of course, I'll be there."

"Thanks," Shelby says before she turns toward the church. This time, Meredith's hand does connect with my shoulder. My big coat mostly blocks her slap, but I still feel it. She points at me, but doesn't say anything before walking away. I'm left standing in the parking lot with just about every member of the congregation staring at me.

Great!

TWENTY-ONE

DELANEY

*I*t's been a week since Fish and I spent the night together, stranded because of the storm. I wish I could say I haven't thought about him, but there's no use in lying to myself. The two almost kisses continue to replay in my mind. I wish I could remember the taste of his lips, but I don't. I've spent the last week pestering Dominic with questions about Aiden, wondering if he's dated since his wife passed away. I'm curious when I shouldn't be. Eager to see him and when all we can be is friends. Desperate to run into him again, almost as if it's a game between us. Yet, I have to remind myself, Aiden and I live completely different lifestyles and thousands of miles away from each other and a winter romance is something neither of us need right now.

My dad and I walk through the park with our boots kicking up the freshly fallen snow. The park is now this magical kingdom of happiness just in time for the winter festival to begin. People from all over the state are here to sell their homemade goods, mingle with people they only see a few times a year and to have fun.

Since my father's election as mayor, he has really transformed our sleepy, cozy little town into somewhere fairytale like, and made the festival into one of the "must-see" events around the state. People from as far as New Hampshire, Massachusetts and Canada flock to take part.

In my teens, the festival used to be my favorite winter event, followed by the town's ice hockey game. This was really the only time I could hit Dominic, if we were lucky enough to be on opposite teams, and get away with it. While I enjoy ice-skating, hockey is something I'd rather watch, and my parents knew this. Yet, they encouraged me to play in this one game.

The booth my father asked me to work at today stands before me. My name is etched onto an arch above the window, and below it says, "Meet and Greet" and there are stanchions set up. The plan is to hand out tickets so I'm not stuck here all night. I want to enjoy the festival as well. Never in my career has my dad asked me for anything special until the other day, but I'm happy to do this for him.

"What do you think?" Dad asks Calvin and me. I'm more concerned with what Calvin has to say since it's his job to protect me.

"How's this going to work?" Calvin asks.

"Well, I'm going to sit in the booth and give every good looking guy a kiss!" I glance at both men, watching their faces morph into anger and regret. "Just kidding," I say.

"I was about to cancel this booth," Dad adds. "Anyway, people will line up at the opening. Everyone must have a ticket, which they can get at the information booth. Delaney will meet with people for two hours each night."

"And what about photos?" Calvin asks. "If she's in the booth, it might be sort of hard."

"People can lean in or whatever," I tell Calvin. "Some

may not want a photo." My dad and Calvin look at me doubtfully and I shrug.

Calvin checks out the structure, making sure it's sturdy enough to withstand the onslaught of people that will be coming toward me. There's a small space heater inside, meant to keep me warm. I appreciate the thought because it's downright cold right now. Not all the top winter gear can keep the chill away, unfortunately.

Of course, each time I shiver, my mind races to Trey and how I should be on the beach, basking under the warmth of the sun, not freezing in the frozen tundra. I don't want to think about him and what he's doing, but I can't help it. I let him walk all over me because I was lonely and the only positive thing that has come out of it is being home. And Aiden, although he shouldn't be a reason, since I haven't seen or spoken to him since I left his house. I was at church that morning, listening to people talk about us. I thought about standing up and telling everyone that they had it wrong, but my mother told me it wouldn't do any good.

"Everything looks good here," Calvin says after he's finished his inspection. "Now what?"

"Now," my dad says, pointing toward the front of the park. "We kick off the holiday season right." Calvin and I follow my dad toward the town Christmas tree. It's been the same one we've decorated for as long as I can remember. People line up at the trellis lit with white lights, when they could easily go around the trees and enter the park that way. However, they respect my father and do as he's asked.

My dad takes his place behind a podium. My mom is there and she pulls me into a half hug. Dominic and Calvin shake hands before Dom takes his place next to Mom, with Calvin behind me. Dad motions for the first couple of people to come through, opening the floodgates. Behind us, carolers start to sing, bringing a huge grin to my father's face. I think this is my dad's favorite part of being mayor.

"Good evening. I'm happy to see so many familiar faces, as well as some I haven't seen before. To you, I say welcome to Ramona Falls. As you may or may not know, actress and my beautiful daughter, Delaney Du Luca is here and will be in the booth right over there," he pauses and points to his right. "Signing autographs and taking pictures. Behind me, our holiday vendors are set-up and ready for business. Don't forget to pick up your apple pie or one of Mrs. Beasley's scarves. They keep the winter chill away. Now without much further ado." Dad turns and faces us. The four of us together put our hands on the light switch and flip it up. The tree bursts into an array of color. Everyone in the crowd oohs and aahs before they start clapping.

Once the tree is lit and people start dispersing, Calvin takes me by the arm and leads me through the maze of people. This is really the first time he's had to work since he arrived. He's different now, more gruff and unforgiving to people who are in his way. While we were busy with the tree lighting someone was kind enough to turn on the space heater, and while I may be toasty warm, Calvin surely isn't. Not that he'd complain. He takes his post outside, standing in front of my booth with one hand clasped over the other, his shoulder square and his head tilted back slightly, causing his chin to jut out. Calvin looks mean, but I think he's nothing more than a giant teddy bear.

For two hours, I sign my name on anything from a napkin to pictures of myself from various magazines. One woman brought in every ticket stub from my movies and had them in a nice shadow box, which she insisted I sign. I was hesitant, fearing I would ruin her project, but she was adamant.

When I see Fish standing among the rest of the people in line, my hand writes a bit faster and I'm shooing people along more quickly. It's finally his turn. He smiles and looks down at Holly, who is beaming ear to ear with one of the biggest grins I have seen all week.

"Delaney," she says as she rushes toward my booth. "I've missed you."

"You saw me the other day at school," I remind her, although our encounter was brief as we were rehearsing for the play.

"But it's not the same."

No, it's definitely not because I'd give anything to be at her house, wrapped in a blanket with her on my lap, listening to her read me a story or singing me her favorite Christmas song.

"I'm so glad you're here," I tell her, avoiding all eye contact with Aiden. I fear if I look at him, I'll see the turmoil he's been going through.

"Why?" Holly asks.

Because I like your daddy. "Because we need a picture together. Would you like that?"

Her head bobs up and down so fast I fear it may pop off. "O.M.Geeeeee," she squeals. I have no choice but to look at Aiden to make sure he's okay, not that I'd expect him to have a problem with us taking a photo together, but some parents are leery.

This time though, I step out of my little box and come around to the front. A few people who are standing on the outside of my roped area try to make a mad dash, but Calvin is there to create a barricade. I crouch down next to Holly and place my arm around her waist, pulling her closer. I haven't done this with any other fans today. I don't know what possesses me to do this with her, maybe it's because she's Aiden's daughter and I want him to know... well, I'm not exactly sure what I want Aiden to know. Part of me wants to spend more time with him, but the logical part of me wants to keep my distance so neither of us gets hurt. Especially, Aiden because he's already been through so much with losing his wife.

Holly and I pose for her dad. He smiles the entire time he's snapping pictures. When he finally drops his camera, I stand, but don't take my hand off of Holly. She looks up at me, smiling. I hope I'm giving her something to hang onto because she's definitely giving me something.

"What are you guys doing later?"

Aiden shakes his head slightly. "Nothing, really. Hanging out around here, I guess."

"You're my last visitor."

"I know, I planned it that way," he says quietly.

"Would you like to get some hot cocoa?" My voice cracks like a school girl asking her crush to check yes or no on the note she just handed him.

"Dad, can we, please?" Holly asks. She jumps up and down with her hands clasped together.

"Yeah, sure. I mean, we're all here." Aiden glances at me quickly before he looks at his daughter. Her excitement is infectious and I find my inner-self jumping up and down too, not because of the cocoa, but because I want to spend more time with the both of them. It takes me only a minute or so to close up my booth, making sure the space heater is unplugged and the light above my name is off.

"Does Mrs. Cline still have the best hot chocolate?" I ask, walking side-by-side with Holly in the middle and Calvin following behind.

"She does," Fish says. Mrs. Cline melts chocolate into milk to make her cocoa. It's thick and frankly, the best I've ever had.

Aiden leads us down the aisle where Mrs. Cline's stand is. When she sees us coming, her smile widens. "Delaney, it's so good to see you."

"You too, Mrs. Cline. We'll take four of your best," I tell her. Absentmindedly, I place my hand on Holly's shoulder and pull her closer to me. I feel like I'm already part of her life.

We're handed our Styrofoam cups and sent along our way. She refuses payment, which I don't like, and will make sure Calvin stops by later to leave her a donation. With Holly's hand in mine, we stop at each table to look at the goods. Aiden isn't far behind us, spending time with Calvin. Those two are chatting it up like they've been best friends for years, while Holly and I continue to bond over hand-made crafts, funny hats and fluffy scarves.

Each time I look over my shoulder, Aiden's eyes are on me. Knowing he's staring causes me to blush, and I like it. Right now, I feel like I'm part of this little family, that they've opened their hearts and lives to accept me, and honestly, it's the best feeling in the world.

TWENTY-TWO

AIDEN

*A*s I expected, Holly's enamored with Delaney from the get-go. Honestly, it'd take a miracle for anyone in Delaney's presence not to be mesmerized by her. Her smile is infectious. She's gracious and humble. Standing there watching her with her fans tonight, was vastly different from the day at the mall. The Delaney I see tonight is caring, and each fan has her undivided attention.

The Laney I know though, is beautiful, loving and the sweetest woman I know, and I'm falling for her, even when I know I shouldn't. I had the hardest time trying to explain to Holly the reason I was waiting to buy the last ticket to see Delaney. Each excuse I thought of was lame and telling her the truth would make me admit, aloud, that my feelings are crossing over the friendship line. The plain truth is, I wanted Holly and I to be the last so we could spend the rest of the night with Delaney.

The other day at church, I came to the realization that my life is not my own. My sister insists on dictating every-thing, including my love life. I know she means well. I know she loves us and would do whatever she could to see us happy. However, I can't help what my heart feels and right now it's pulling me in the direction of Delaney Du Luca, knowing full well that once the holidays are over, she'll be gone. I can only hope and pray Delaney doesn't forget us.

Currently, my daughter and the woman I'm fawning over are lying in the snow, making snow angels. Calvin and I are standing so we can block the girls from the public eye. Secretly, I'm thankful for his presence. I think with Calvin here, it allows Delaney to have more freedom, and it definitely makes me aware of my surroundings. I only wish we had protected her enough that Delaney didn't even have to call Calvin to come rescue her.

Their giggles carry over the park, causing me to smile. It's been so long since Holly has seemed this carefree, and I have Delaney to thank. I wish I could capture this moment on film, but I know Laney would hate it.

Calvin turns and watches the crowd intently while I keep my eyes on the girls, trying to burn the vision of them together into my mind.

"What happened the other night?" Calvin asks.

"Don't know what you mean."

He clears his throat and steps to his side, pushing his shoulder into mine. "I wanted to come get her, but she refused. I didn't think anything of it until the next afternoon when she was crying her eyes out."

"Crying?"

"Hmh," he mumbles. "Suppose you don't know why she was doing that?"

I shake my head. When she left my house, everything was good, minus my nosy neighbor stopping us before we could kiss. The thought of her crying though, I don't like that.

"You mean something to her. But if you're not sure…"

His words stab me in the heart. Deep down, he's right, I'm guarded when it comes to my heart. Laney has a lot to offer... someone. Unfortunately, as much as I want to be that someone, I'm not sure I can.

"Laney is a good friend. We have a small history, but who doesn't when you grow up in a small town?"

Calvin gives me the side eye and I quickly tear my gaze away from him. The girls come over to us, walking hand in hand, covered head to toe in snow. Their noses and cheeks are red, hair matted with snowballs and their clothes are soaked. "You guys are going to catch your death," I say, pulling Holly into my arms.

"You sound like a grandma," Laney says, and Holly laughs.

"He does sound like my grandma."

"What do you say we go to my house and warm up by the fire?" Delaney suggests. I'm about to tell her we'll take a rain check until Holly starts jumping up and down, clapping her hands.

"Daddy, can we *please*?" she clasps her hands together in a praying motion, juts out her bottom lip and bats her eyelashes which have the tiniest of snowflakes on them. This is my weakness and she knows it.

I look from Holly to Delaney, whose expression all but matches Holly's and it hits me I can't say no to either of them. However, I'm going to try. "I don't know. It's getting late, I'm sure Mr. and Mrs. Du Luca are tired."

"Fish, you know very well my parents aren't leaving here until the last person has left for the night. Come on, it'll be like old times." Laney's hand rests on my arm and the tingling from the other day is back with a vengeance.

"Old times, Daddy?" Holly asks. Her face is scrunched, a sure sign of confusion. I'm shocked that word hasn't spread to my daughter about the time I dated her favorite movie star. Maybe I should've used this to my advantage the other day when she was yelling at me in the lunchroom at school.

My gaze diverts from Laney's. She shrugs and smiles, sealing my fate. Even if I wanted to say no, I couldn't. The fight on my hands wouldn't be worth it. Not from Delaney or Holly.

"We'll follow you over," I tell Delaney.

"Yes! Can I ride with Delaney?" Holly asks.

"I don't—"

"It's fine," Delaney says. "Calvin is an excellent driver. Nothing will happen to her, Fish. I promise." Laney reaches for Holly's hand and my instinct is to pull Holly away, but I don't. My daughter's hand rests in Delaney's, both of their faces beam brightly with smiles as they start to walk away. I have no choice but to follow along, walking step-by-step with Calvin.

"You'll learn to just give in," he says.

I shake my head. "The newness of Delaney will wear off and Holly will move onto something else."

"I wasn't talking about Holly." Calvin rushes to his black SUV, which sticks out in town like a sore thumb, leaving me there to ponder his words. He doesn't wait for me to make up my mind about what I'm going to do, and pulls away from the curb with my daughter in the back of his car.

Almost in a full jog, I hurry to my car for no other reason than to follow behind. It's not like I don't know where the Du Lucas live or am afraid I might miss something. No, that's not entirely true. I am afraid. I'm afraid I'm going to miss Holly laughing so hard tears will come out of her eyes. I'm scared to miss the memories she's building tonight with Delaney and I won't be able to remind her of them when she's older because her mind is too young to remember. I'm nervous Holly will break something and feel like she's in trouble if I'm not there to ease her mind. Most of all I'm anxious to spend time with Laney. It's stupid, but since I pulled her over, I've been saying what if.

By the time I arrive at the Du Luca's, everyone is already in the house. I knock before opening the door, much like I used to when I was coming over years ago. From the foyer, I can hear laughter and Christmas music. As quickly as I can, I take off my winter wear, kick off my boots and walk into the kitchen.

Delaney's crouched down with her head in the cupboard and blindly handing Holly large mixing bowls and baking sheets. Laney doesn't even look my way before heading to the pantry. She's listing off the ingredients for what I'm assuming will be the best tasting cookies ever.

"Care for a drink?" Calvin asks as he steps next to me.

"What're having?"

"Eggnog. Adult style."

I glance at Holly and Delaney, realizing I'll be here for a bit so a little adult beverage won't hurt. "Sure." I follow Calvin to the butler's pantry and take my glass after he fills it part way. "You seem to know your way around the Du Luca's."

"Mr. D gave me a crash course and told me if I didn't make myself at home, he'd have me arrested. I took his threat seriously when Dominic came over."

I chuckle. "Dom is all talk, no bite."

Calvin doesn't seem to believe me, but that doesn't surprise me. Calvin's demeanor doesn't seem to change much. I can't tell if he's enjoying his drink or not. "There should be a game on," I say to him, figuring watching some sporting event might get him to open up.

He follows me into the den, where I flip on the television and change the sports channel to basketball. The score's tied, and the announcers for the Celtics are going crazy with the back and forth between the Cs and Cavs. Growing up, I counted the days until the Celtics would vie for another championship. It was only after they traded for Kevin Garnett and Ray Allen things changed. Now, we're on the cusp of greatness again.

I enjoy sports as much as any other guy, but since Heather's passing, they've taken a backseat. There was a time when I'd meet up with my friends at the local pub to watch one of the many Boston teams play, but those days are long over. I didn't think I missed it until now.

Calvin and I take turns yelling at the TV, throwing our hands up in the air and flopping back on the couch when a call doesn't go our way.

"What's all this noise?"

Calvin and I both turn our heads at the scolding voice of Delaney. Standing next to her, mimicking her stance is Holly. They're both glaring at us, with their hands on their hips. Instantly, I'm taken back by the way Delaney and Holly look. If I didn't know better, I'd say my wife and daughter were standing in front of me, and it knocks the breath out of me, because having those thoughts is wrong.

When I look at Holly, I see Heather. They're spitting images of each other, but right now she's a mini Delaney. They both have their hair in buns, are wearing headbands, aprons, and both seem to have flour all over their faces. Holly looks at me, as if I've done something wrong.

"What?" I ask. Delaney crosses her arms, followed quickly by Holly.

"There's a whole lotta yelling going on in here."

"The game's on. You know how it is," I point to the screen.

"Well, we thought you guys would like some cookies," Holly says in her best Delaney impersonation. She's a real mini Laney right now.

"Now you're speaking my language." Calvin stands and makes his way into the kitchen. I start to follow, but am held tightly under Delaney's penetrating gaze.

"Can I help you?" Delaney asks as I step closer. In doing so, Holly does as well, almost as if she's preventing me from being near Delaney.

"You have something here." My finger brushes along her skin. The white powdery flour does nothing to conceal the red rosy coloring of her cheek. Delaney's fingers squeeze my side, her nails digging into my flesh.

"And what would that be, Fish?"

Holly laughs. "Daddy, she called you Fish again."

"Because it's my name," I say.

"And what's mine?" Delaney asks.

"Laney." Her name escapes breathlessly through my lips. I step closer, my lips poised to touch her. She swallows hard, waiting for me to make a move.

"Daddy, do you want a cookie or not?" Holly sounds exasperated by my not so subtle attempts at flirting. Delaney drops her hand from my side and steps back, putting some space between us.

It takes a few seconds to clear my thoughts. Twice now, I've wanted to kiss Delaney. However, we were somewhat hidden. Tonight though, my daughter is standing between us, preventing me from making a mistake. Yet, knowing she's there does nothing to help the images I have of pulling Delaney into my arms and pressing my lips to her.

I finally break away from Delaney's gaze to look at Holly. "Yes, Holly, I want a cookie or two, maybe even three."

"No way," she says, running back into the kitchen. Delaney and I stand there in awkward silence until we hear Holly yell. "No, Calvin, you can't eat all the cookies!"

TWENTY-THREE

DELANEY

Sometime around midnight, my parents come home. They're loud, boisterous and, it seems, ready to party. I look around our family room to find Holly curled up on the couch, Aiden passed out next to her and Calvin asleep in the recliner. There's some infomercial on about a special glue that will hold anything playing on the TV, and I find myself wanting to buy it to try it out.

Luckily, the noise from the party animals is enough to wake everyone, except for Holly. Honestly, I think the girl ate so many cookies she's in a food coma after her sugar crash. Aiden stretches and his shirt rises a little, showing off a small sliver of skin. I look away and giggle. The action is completely school girlish, but I don't care.

"What's going on in here?" my mom asks as she comes into the room, making eye contact with each of us. I watch as she pauses on Holly before turning attention to Aiden. "Hello, Aiden." She draws out his name, almost as if she's surprised to see him. She shouldn't be since I've done nothing but talk about him since I spent the night at his house. Sure, it was more of me talking to myself, listing all the reason why I should friend zone Aiden, and her listening, providing me reasons why I should give love a chance, and how Aiden and I deserve happiness.

Thing is, we do deserve happiness, but maybe not with each other. I know I have a lot to offer him and Holly, but I also come with baggage. I'm gone for months on end. My hours are horrible. My life is constantly under scrutiny. Although, after his neighbor blabbed to the entire town that she saw us making-out, his life is too. The worse part is that Aiden and I weren't doing anything wrong or anything at all for that matter.

"Hi, Mrs. Du Luca," he says groggily. Aiden sits up and rubs his hands over his face. He offers my mom a quick smile before turning his attention Holly.

"Do you want some help?" I ask, even though I have no idea what I'm going to do to help.

"Why doesn't she stay here?" Mom offers.

"Thanks for the offer, Ms. Du Luca, but I'll take her home. We have a big day tomorrow."

"Yes, I suppose we're all so busy with the festival."

"And we have the policeman's Christmas party next week," Aiden reminds her. "Surely, you haven't forgotten."

"Oh, of course not. The Women's Guild has been busy wrapping presents for all the children. Santa is so excited to be there. It'll be so much fun."

It's been years since I've been to the ball. When we were teenagers, we had cleanup duty since we were too old to participate. Nevertheless, I remember going when I was younger to sit on Santa's lap. He always seemed to know what I wanted.

Aiden scoops Holly up and I follow him to the door, where I help him slide Holly's coat on. "She's out cold."

"You fed her too many cookies," he says, causing me to step away.

"I didn't mean to say it like that. She had a lot of fun here, Laney. I haven't seen her this happy in a long time and that's because of you."

"She's a great little girl, Aiden. I really..." Do I like her? Care for her? Love her as if she were my own?

"I know," he says, filling in my missing words with whatever works for his life. I open the door for them and follow them out into the cold night air without a jacket. Aiden hurries to put Holly into the truck and runs around to the driver's side to start it. He closes the door and comes over to me, using his hands to rub up and down my arms before pulling me into his embrace. "I had the best time tonight. I don't know how I'll ever be able to thank you for making Holly's Christmas so magical. She hasn't stopped talking about you since you came over the other night."

"She's amazing, Aiden."

"So are you. And Calvin... I'm glad you brought him here. I've enjoyed getting to know him."

Is Aiden deflecting? Is he hiding his feelings from me by bringing up Calvin? "You and Calvin seem to be good friends."

"He's great. He really cares for you, Delaney."

Does Aiden think Calvin has a thing for me? I certainly hope not. Relationships between employee and employer are common, especially in my industry, but Calvin is my best friend. He's my confidant when I need to unload. He's my protector when I have no one else. "Yeah, he is. He's my best friend in Los Angeles. Honestly, I'd be a hermit if it weren't for him." I adjust slightly so I can look at Aiden, hoping he can see in my eyes, what I'm telling him.

"He told me you were crying the other day. Why?" Aiden looks concerned.

"I don't even remember, actually. Probably something Dominic did to me. You know how he is." I shake my head, hoping to convey my tears were for nothing. He doesn't need to know I heard people talking about him and how he was romancing another woman until I arrived. Aiden and I may not have stayed in touch, but I can't imagine his character has changed over the years. The Aiden Fisher I know isn't a cad.

Aiden brushes over my cheek with the back of his hand. Our eyes never leave each other's. We're so close. If I were to rise up on my tippy toes, I could kiss him right here and now, but not with Holly in the truck. I don't want to put Aiden in a situation where he has to explain why he's kissing someone other than her mommy. "Goodnight," I say, stepping out of his grasp.

Aiden pulls me back to him and kisses my forehead. His warm lips linger, burning into my skin, my thoughts and my heart. I close my eyes and wish for a time when everything would be perfect. Sadly, a time like that existed ten years ago. Things could've been different for the both of us or we could've easily ended up like many of the other failed relationships. It's hard not knowing if you made one change in your life, how different things could be.

I step away and head into my parents' house. I do so without looking back to see if he's watching. I want to think he is and want that to be my last thought of the night. Inside, the house is quiet, but the glow from the television tells me someone is still awake. In the den, my father's in his recliner flipping through the channels.

"Hey." I sit on the couch, choosing the spot closest to my dad.

"Aiden gone?"

"Yeah, he is."

"You know he waited in line for a ticket to see you tonight. Told Maryann he wanted the last two."

"I heard. I'm not sure why though. All he had to do is ask me to meet him."

Dad sets the remote down and looks at me. "You know sometimes men like to take things slow. I know in your world, everything moves at such speed, but here we like to stop and smell the roses."

"It's winter. There are no roses, unless men have some magical garden us women don't know about, in which case you should start sharing because I know Mom loves red roses, especially at Christmastime."

My dad gives me the side eye and a sly grin. I just nailed one of the gifts my mom will receive in the next few days. For as long as I can remember, my dad has given my mom a gift every day during the week leading up to Christmas. I've always wanted this type of love and I'm still waiting to find it.

"What I'm saying, dear daughter of mine, is sometimes us men like to take things slow. We want to enjoy the chase. We want our victory to be sweet."

"You make love sound like a game."

"Isn't it though?" he asks. "Where's the fun in walking up to a beautiful woman and saying 'I want to take you on a date?'"

"Sometimes being forward is the best way," I counter.

Dad shakes his head. "Nah. Sometimes getting to know the person you're interested in makes dating so much sweeter."

"Why are we having this conversation? It's not like Aiden and I are going to start dating."

"Oh!"

I roll my eyes, knowing he can't see them in the dark and won't be able to chastise me for it. "Aiden and I come from two different worlds, as you mentioned. At the end of the month, I go back to my crazy, hectic life, and he stays here protecting the people of Ramona Falls and raising his daughter. I would never wish my lifestyle on him and Holly, and although Holly would love the glitz and glam, I don't think Aiden would. Everything about my world is unpredictable and somewhat scary. I have a bodyguard for a reason. Being under the scrutiny of people, twenty-four seven is tiring. Aiden wouldn't want this type of life."

"Have you asked him?"

I scoff. "Daddy, we're not dating. We're not even seeing each other. We're hanging out, being friends and enjoying what little time I have here. Besides, the rumor around town is he already has eyes for another woman, and I'm probably in the way, always inserting myself into his life."

"You can't listen to everything you hear around town, Delaney. If I did, I'd worry about whether or not I'm doing a good job."

"But you are."

"According to you, I am. However, not everyone feels the same as you. People like to stir pots." He closes his recliner and gets up, handing me the remote. "Listen, all I'm saying is, things aren't as they always seem. If a man is willing to buy the last two tickets to see someone, and wait in the freezing cold for his turn, he may be worth the chance." Dad kisses me on top of my head and ruffles my hair. "Goodnight, dear. See you at your booth in the morning."

Ugh! Personal appearances on a lack of sleep never bode well for me. Still instead of going to bed, I lie on the couch and continue to flip through the channels until I land on the *Sound of Music*. For the life of me, I'll never understand why this is a Christmas movie. No one sings any Christmas carols. There isn't a tree, presents or even snow and it takes place in Austria, which surely has snow in the wintertime. I just don't get it, yet here it is, on TV, before the holiday. I still watch it, though, and sing along to every song. Living here though has afforded many of us to grow up with the Von Trapps. I've even asked their great-grand children why their family's movie is mostly shown at Christmas and they don't understand it either.

When the movie ends, I drag myself to my bedroom and fall onto my bed without changing my clothes. I do remember to set my alarm for the morning though, which then has me looking at Aiden's contact information. Is my dad right? Does Aiden want to pursue something with me? I press the icon to send him a message and start typing.

I'm often up late at night even when I have to be some-place early in the morning. I don't know why I'm writing to you or if you're even awake, but I am. Thank you for letting Holly come over tonight. She's such an amazing little girl and I had the best time making cookies with her. Spending time with the both of you has been the best present a girl could ask for. Hopefully, I'll see you tomorrow. If not, enjoy your weekend, Aiden. ~ Laney.

I hit send before I can chicken out, and watch as the message delivers. I read it over, wondering if I should've said something different, but it's too late. What's done is done.

TWENTY-FOUR

AIDEN

*W*hen my phone chimed in the middle of the night, I was wide-awake, thinking about Delaney. Telling myself I'm only imagining the feelings I'm having and there's no way she's feeling the same. Her message changed everything. It wasn't a declaration of love, or a plea for us to take things to the next level, but a heartfelt note, which has given me clarity. The problem is, I don't know what to do with it, which is evident by the way I've avoided the winter festival all day until now.

As soon as I pull into the parking lot by the town's ice rink, Holly jumps out of the truck. Her friend Shawna is waving rapidly for Holly to join her. The girls take off running toward the rink, both falling multiple times in the knee-deep snow.

"I think they'll be best friends for life." The voice of Shelby catches me off guard, causing me to drop my gear onto the pavement.

"Yeah, Holly talks very fondly about Shawna."

"We would like to invite you over for dinner tonight."

I run my hand over my stocking cap and nod. I'm not

good at telling people no, and I know Holly would like some more time with Shawna. "That sounds nice."

"Holly is more than welcome to spend the night." Shelby falls in step next to me as I make my way toward the rink where there are a few people already warming up for our game.

"Yeah, sure. I think she'd like that."

Shelby starts to slip, and I catch her easily. Her hand lands on my forearm and mine ends up around her waist. She licks her lips and smiles. "Thank you. You're my hero."

I nod again and step back, putting some space between us. Shelby doesn't though, and links her arm with mine, holding onto me until we get to the rink. Being the gentleman I am, I make sure she's at the bleachers before jumping over the wall.

"Shelby Whittensby, huh?" James Alvarez holds out his fist for me to bump. I don't. Instead, I look over my shoulder to find Shelby staring at me. She gives me a little finger wave, but it's the sound of Holly yelling out Delaney's name that has my attention focused elsewhere.

"Nothing going on there," I tell James, who happens to be on the force with me. He and his wife moved here a few years back when he was hired. "Our daughters are friends."

"That's not what she's been telling my wife."

"Can't listen to everything you hear."

James slaps me on the back. "She's the most eligible woman in town. You'd be a fool not to be with her."

Then call me a fool because the attraction isn't there. Sure, Shelby is beautiful, but she comes on too strong and I don't like that quality in a woman. Not to mention, she talks a lot about me as if we're dating when we're not. I've been over to her house once for dinner and nothing happened. Still, according to my sister, I've upset Shelby because supposedly Delaney and I were making out. This town, I swear.

"Sorry to disappoint you, Alvarez, but there's nothing going on between us."

"Does *she* know this?" He points over his shoulder, which causes me to turn around and see her in the stands, holding a sign with my name on it. Not only that, but Delaney sees the same sign and immediately looks at me, with an expression I can't decipher. I open my mouth to talk to her, but she heads over to the other bench without giving me a second glance.

"Wonderful," I mutter as I slip into my pads.

"Ah, I get it now," James says. "You and the actress."

"That's my sister you're talking about, Alvarez."

James holds his hands up. "No harm, Du Luca. Only making an observation."

Dominic grunts as he sits down. I pull my skates on and bend over to tie them while Dom continues to make unintelligible sounds. "What's up?"

"You tell me. Delaney has been in a bad mood all day and warned me to stay away from her on the ice or I'm 'going to get it.'"

I look down the bench to find her talking with Calvin, who thankfully isn't changing into any hockey gear. I can't imagine him on skates. It'd be like going against Chára and I don't think my body can handle it.

With my skates tied, I hit the ice for a few warm-up laps. Tomorrow, I'm going to be hurting. I haven't skated or played hockey since last year's game, and honestly I spent most of the time on the bench because I wasn't feeling it. It was our first Christmas without Heather and I had to force myself to feel the festive spirit when all I wanted to do was wallow in self-pity from losing my wife. Except when you have a child to look after, you can't. It wouldn't be fair to let her lose the magic of Christmas.

I come to a skid in front of Delaney, spraying ice shavings all over her skates. Her hands pause, but only for a second. I expect her to look up or push me away from her, but she does neither. "What's up?" I sit down next to her, our shoulders touching, only for her to stand and skate away.

Dom stops in front of me, blocking my view of Delaney. "Man, what did you do?"

"Nothing!" I throw my hands up in the air.

"You sure? Because she's upset and clearly at you."

My knees wobble a bit as I stand. "Why? What'd I do?"

Dominic shrugs. "Don't know, but I have a feeling she's going to take it out on you once the game starts." He skates away, leaving me there to watch Delaney and Mindy as they practices hitting the puck into the net. Every so often, Mindy looks over and glares. Perfect.

MY BODY'S SORE. It aches in places I didn't know existed. Never mind the fact that I have bruises where I shouldn't. I blame Delaney and Mindy. Every chance they had to hit me, they did. It was a tag team effort and one they executed flawlessly.

At the end of the first period, I yelled for a team switch, but the girls refused to be on my team. That's when I knew I was their target. The reason – I still have no idea but it didn't matter where I was on the ice, they were coming after me. And forget it if I had the puck, they gladly took their penalties and sat in the sin bin for cross checking and tripping. I swear I think I saw Mindy and Delaney high-five each other after I went flying into the boards, head first no less.

What's worse I promised Holly we'd go over to Shawna's for dinner. I'm all for her staying the night because it gives me a chance to sleep off the pain but I'm not in the mood to stay. I don't care if Shelby is a good cook. I have a feeling she's the one spreading rumors about our non-existent relationship, and I have no idea how to approach her about that. The last thing I want to do is upset her, but on the other hand I need her to stop.

The hot spray from the shower does nothing to ease away the throbbing in my muscles. It might be time to face facts; I'm too old for this. Or I'm too old to play when Delaney is in town. I know it's been ten years since I've seen her play, but I don't remember her being this violent.

I gingerly dry off, careful not to twist the wrong way. I can hear Holly singing Christmas songs, loudly and out of tune, but still I smile. She's the best part of me, which is why I'll keep my promise to her and go over to Shawna's. As much as I want to drop her off, I also don't want to be rude. We were invited to dinner and I said we'd go. If anything, I'm a man who keeps my word.

After dressing and making sure Holly's overnight bag is packed, we make one stop at the store to buy our host flowers or a thank you gift. My parents raised me right and never allowed me to show up empty handed. Although, bringing flowers might send the wrong message so Holly and I decide on a poinsettia. It's Christmas and everyone seems to like them.

Shawna is staring out their big picture window when we pull up. Holly, once again, bolts from the truck before I have a chance to even shut it off. She's inside and running around when I rap my knuckles on the door before stepping in.

"In here," Shelby yells out from her kitchen. I walk in with her poinsettia in one hand and Holly's bag in another.

"This is for you." I present the red cellophane potted plant to her. Shelby steps forward, her hand touches mine and lingers there for a minute.

"This is beautiful. I know the perfect place for it." I follow her out of the kitchen and into the living room where she sets our gift down on her end table. Her tree catches my attention. It's bare, other than a string of lights.

"You don't have any decorations on your tree." I point out the obvious.

Shelby giggles. "We're decorating tonight."

"Oh, Holly will love that."

"Hopefully, you will too. I thought we could do it together."

It's not very often I'm rendered speechless, but here I am, stunned into silence. Decorating a family tree should be something families do together. With that said, I know Delaney was there helping with mine, but I've known her for years and when we were younger I was often at the Du Luca's and spent many holiday eves there. *This* though, screams relationship status and I'm not entirely comfortable with it.

"Um..."

"It'll be fun and the girls will love it."

Think about Holly, I tell myself. "Yes, I'm sure they will. Speaking of, where should I put her bag?" I hold it up to show Shelby it's still in my hand.

"Follow me." Shelby takes us to Shawna's room where the girls are coloring. Holly doesn't even notice I'm in the room, but does say hi to me. "The girls play so well together." Shelby places one hand on my forearm and the other on my stomach.

As casual as possible, I step away from her and go to Holly under the premise I want to see what she's coloring. Delaney's name is in the top right corner. The thought of Holly coloring something for Delaney brings a smile to face.

"Dinner's about ready, girls. Go wash up," Shelby tells them. Both girls hop to it, chatting the whole way to the bathroom.

"Do you need help?" I ask, trying to be polite.

Shelby shakes her head. "Just make yourself at home, Aiden."

Home. It's where I want to be right now, but instead I'm lingering near the bathroom door, using my daughter as an excuse so I'm not caught off guard by Shelby. I shouldn't feel like this. Shelby's a beautiful woman, but not the right one for me. Or maybe she is and I'm just too blind to see it? Would I be in a relationship with Shelby had Delaney not come back? The question weighs heavily on my mind as I trail behind the girls. Unfortunately, I don't know the answer and it's not like I can ask my best friend or sister for advice. Dominic will tease me relentlessly and Meredith will tell me to do the right thing and date Shelby. Not because she's the safest option, but probably because she's the only option. I'm a fool to think Delaney will ever be anything more than a friend.

TWENTY-FIVE

DELANEY

I don't know why I ever look at social media. There's always something posted that will inevitably upset me. Today, it's the post Shelby Whittensby made a few nights ago, showing the world aka Ramona Falls, a picture of her, her daughter, Holly and Aiden, posing together in front of her tree. I know it's her tree because I had the privilege of decorating Aiden's. Was it a privilege or did I invite myself to take part in something he was doing with his daughter because I wanted to be there? I've been asking myself this question ever since this picture was posted. I hate second-guessing myself as much as I hate the hashtags Shelby added to her post: family, Christmas and love.

Love, really? Are they in love or does she just love the photo? It's really hard to tell because his arm is around her and they look happy. So ridiculously happy, the sight of them makes my stomach hurt. She's pretty and perfect for him, and I'm envious. Jealous because I thought Aiden and I had something and I'm bothered by his relationship with Shelby because we almost kissed, twice or was it three times? Was I misreading the situation or did he realize I'm no good for him so he's doing what's right for his family?

"Will you stop looking at your phone?" Mindy hisses across the table. Calvin chuckles, but otherwise doesn't say anything. The restaurant we're in is full, and I've already been approached for autographs, which I signed of course, but refused to pose for pictures. I'd like to be left alone while on vacation, but being back home means I have to be a bit flexible.

"I can't help it, Min. Look at them!" I turn the screen so she can see the same picture I've been showing her non-stop since it appeared on her timeline. Mindy may be my best friend, but she liked the photo because it's the nice "town" thing to do. "You should've used the mad emoji or something."

"You're being petty."

I roll my eyes and take a sip of my wine. "I'm not."

"You are," Calvin chimes in. "You're not dating him and in a few weeks you'll be back in California, forgetting everyone and everything in Ramona Falls. Let the man find a bit of happiness."

I glare at Calvin, hating the fact that he's right. After Christmas, I have to go back, even though I intended to stay until the New Year. The director of my recent project has called for reshoots and since I *conveniently* didn't leave the country, he was able to harass my agent enough, who insisted I return home to get them done.

"Unless you're telling us something else, D. Are you falling for Aiden Fisher?" Mindy's eyes never leave mine as she takes a drink of her wine. I pick mine back up and finish it off, avoiding her question. Calvin laughs, and my kneejerk reaction is to kick him. Thankfully, no one can see under our table, otherwise I'd be all over social media for abusing my bodyguard.

"I'm not saying anything."

"You don't have to. It's written all over your face." Mindy's wrong. I'm stoic when it comes to my emotions. I've learned over the years to hide them, especially from the paparazzi.

Speaking of, the man a few tables away is staring. Each time I look over, he smiles and it takes me a minute to remember I've seen him before. I lean into Calvin and say as quietly as possible, "There's a man two tables over to the left. He looks familiar and this is the second time I've seen him. Where do I know him from?"

Calvin, being not the so subtle man he is, turns in his chair and looks. He's not shy about lingering either or letting the man know he's paying attention to him now. When Calvin turns back to the table, his face pales, which is saying a lot.

"What's wrong?" I ask.

"He's paps."

"What? Are you sure? What's he doing here?" I make an ill-fated attempt at keeping my voice down, but to no avail. The people next to us are now looking. I smile, but know it comes off as a grimace.

"Wait a minute, this is the guy from the lounge the other night. I remember him," Mindy says. "He totally creeped you out, D." I look again and nod because she's right.

"What do you mean?" Calvin asks. He looks from Mindy to me, except when he makes eye contact with me, he's glaring. Oops. I suppose I should've told him.

"I bought him a drink." I hang my head, waiting for Calvin to rip into me. When he doesn't, I glance at him, only to see him seething, trying to keep his temper in check.

"Continue."

"Right, so you guys were at the hockey game and I went out with my mom, Mindy and Eileen. We went to New Hampshire to this cute lounge for some drinks. He was sitting at the bar when I went up to order a drink and I bought him one. He seemed nice, until he looked at me and I felt something off about him."

"You told me you'd stay home."

I reach over and place my hand on top of his. Calvin takes his job very seriously and had he known I was planning to go out, he would've never gone with the guys and I didn't want him to feel like he was just here to work. "I'm sorry. I know and I should've told you, but I honestly didn't think anything of it. But now—"

"But now, he's showing up in other places because I saw him at the festival," Mindy adds. Calvin grumbles something very profane and clenches his jaw. I need to help Mindy understand there's a time and place to drop these kind of bombs. This is definitely not one of those times.

"I can't do my job, Delaney, if you're not being honest with me. It's one thing if you're out with your dad, Dominic or Aiden, but when you're vulnerable with no one to protect you—"

"Hey!" Mindy yells loudly and punches Calvin in the shoulder. This proves to be a mistake since she's shaking her hand out. "We wouldn't let anything happen to her."

"But you wouldn't know to protect her either from someone like him."

Calvin has a point. I never thought the paparazzi would show up here, let alone during the holidays when there are so many more important people to follow around Los

Angeles or in some tropical destination. Who in their right mind visits the land of frozen trees, knee-deep snow and wind chill temperatures below twenty? I wouldn't, not if my family didn't live here.

Calvin excuses himself and goes over to the man. I can't tell what's going on, by the way he's standing, but I have a feeling my bodyguard is telling him exactly where he needs to be and it isn't Ramona Falls. When he comes back, his shoulders are square and he's pulling my chair out. "We're leaving."

"Okay." I know better than to argue with him. Mindy and I grab our things and she drops a few twenties down on the table to pay for our appetizer and drinks. "What about shopping?" I ask, hesitantly. Our plan today was to do some Christmas shopping. We only stopped to have lunch, which has turned out to be a complete failure.

"If you insist, but take this warning to heart. I'm not going to leave your side."

"Duly noted." I thread my arm into his as he leads me to the SUV. Behind me, Mindy is chuckling, at what, I don't know. Maybe she finds it funny that he's actually the boss. I suppose in a sense he is.

Calvin dutifully drives Mindy and I to the outdoor mall. Of course, it's snowing and we have to bundle up. As soon as Mindy and I see Starbucks, we head in for venti peppermint mochas. Calvin says he doesn't want one, but ends up with his own regardless. Deep down, I know he loves them, but will never admit it.

Outside, I spin in a circle with my arms spread out wide and my head tilted back. The white lights that connect from each building light the cobblestone walkway, casting the perfect holiday glow. "I love it here," I say to anyone listening. "Don't you?" I look at Calvin, who's shaking his head.

"Come on, Calvin. It's December, Christmas is in the air and look at the storefronts, they're beautiful, and the music... don't you want to sing?"

"No, Delaney. I want to go inside where it's warm."

"Don't be a scrooge."

"He's right though, D. It's cold. Come on, let's shop. I have kids to buy for."

Grudgingly, I follow behind Calvin and Mindy as if I've been scolded. After making snow angels with Holly the other day, I've had a strong urge to play in the snow. Maybe I missed being home during winter more than I thought.

Our first stop is this cute little kids' store. It's a place I've never been to before, but there's a special little girl in my heart I want to shop for. Mindy gives me a look that I easily brush off. Each dress, tutu, leggings, every little girl item I pick up, I love, and they get added to the pile forming in Calvin's arms.

"You're going overboard," Mindy says as she hands me an outfit her daughter will like. I feel bad I haven't spent anytime with her children yet, but I plan on it. The closer we get to Christmas the more I'll be over at her house, celebrating with them.

With one store down, we stop at another and so on. At each one, I find things Holly needs. Giant teddy bears, tiaras, dolls, every art supply possible. Everything I see, I pick up and hand to Calvin.

"Are you sure Aiden will be okay with this?" he asks after the fifth, sixth or tenth store. We've been to so many now, I've lost count.

"Why wouldn't he be? I'm only picking up a few things."

"A few?" Mindy questions. "I think you've single-handedly helped each store meet their holiday quota for sales."

"I have not."

"You have. I've made three trips to the car already," Calvin says.

"What's your point?"

"*Our...*" Mindy scoffs and points back and forth between Calvin and her. "Point is, Aiden lives a really simple life since Heather died. Holly's going to think everyone is like you, and the sad reality is, they're not."

I understand what Mindy's saying, but I don't want to believe I'm doing anything wrong. The conclusion I come to, is Aiden needs the same treatment. He probably hasn't bought himself anything new since his wife passed away. He's so focused on Holly, he's likely forgetting about himself.

However, I do what my friends suggest and tone it down, even as I continue to shop. Everything I pick up, Mindy and Calvin shake their heads. I finally give up and start buying for my parents and Dominic. Everything Calvin likes, I sneak one in for him and Aiden too.

On the drive home, I sit in the back and stare out the window, tuning the chatter between Calvin and Mindy out. I like the idea of making Holly and Aiden's Christmas better. I have the means to do it, but I don't want him to think I'm trying to come between him and Shelby.

Calvin drops Mindy off at her house, helping her with her packages. I hug her goodbye, telling her I have the festival play this weekend, and she promises to be there. Mindy also reminds me about the policeman's party on Friday night, telling me I should go. I don't know if my presence would be such a good idea, but I don't tell her that.

TWENTY-SIX

AIDEN

*I*f you ever want to know where you stand with Delaney De Luca, don't return or acknowledge her heartfelt text message. This is the mistake I've made, and I'm paying dearly for it. Holly isn't though, since she sees Delaney every day and talks about her non-stop once she's home from school. It's pretty bad I have to get information about Delaney from my seven year old. The problem is, I don't know what to say to Delaney and every time I've tried to approach her, she's smiled politely and turned the other way.

To top everything else off, Shelby posted a photo of us, indicating we are a couple, when that couldn't be further from the truth. I like her, but that's it. My heart doesn't race when she's around, nor do my palms sweat or my skin feel like it's about to jump off my body when she touches me. Those are all things I feel when I'm with Delaney. The worst part is I don't know what to do about it.

There isn't much I can do, honestly. Delaney is leaving at the end of the month, and will go back to her life in California where she's living her dream. I'll be here, raising my daughter and struggling to make ends meet. I'm not jealous. I'm resentful. My life wasn't supposed to be like this. I had everything. A beautiful wife and child, a good job, a happy home, and then someone or some force thought Heather and I could handle the unthinkable. We tried. We fought. We loved until the end.

Now the thought of being in love again looms in front of me and I can't take it. I can't ask Delaney to move here and uprooting Holly is out of the question. My job is here. My parents and sister are here. In Los Angeles, we'd only have Delaney, when she's there. That isn't a lifestyle I want for my daughter.

"Daddy, do you think you can call Laney and ask her to do my hair?" Holly stands before me. Tonight is the annual policeman's holiday dinner and party. It's always been a family oriented event with Santa and Mrs. Claus making an appearance to hand out toys to all the children.

"Aunt Meredith said she'd be over to help."

Holly shakes her head and juts out her lower lip. "I want Laney to do it." She stomps her foot and crosses her arms over her chest.

"I'm sorry, but Delaney is busy." I hate that I've called her anything but her nickname, but I think I'm wise to separate myself from her. Besides, she's made it clear we're nothing more than friends.

"But she promised."

I never want to call my daughter a liar, but I do question whether Delaney said this to her. "Maybe you misunderstood."

"I. Did. Not!"

"Holly, I know you're upset, but I'm sorry, Delaney isn't coming over to do your hair. Aunt Meredith will though."

Holly screeches, like a wild banshee. She's trying to

push me over the edge into yelling at her. *This* is exactly what I knew would happen. Holly would become attached to Delaney, and not understand why Delaney can't be around anytime Holly wants. I'm an adult and even I have a hard time comprehending why I can't have my way when I want it.

"I don't want to go."

I sigh and pinch the bridge of my nose. "You don't want to see Santa and tell him what you want for Christmas?"

"No. I want Delaney."

"You can't have her."

"You're a meanie."

I nod. "And you're acting like a baby, so why don't you go to your room and think about things. When you're ready to talk to me with some respect we can have a conversation." I point toward the hall, which only causes Holly to hold her breath so her face can turn red. Temper tantrums are the highlight of my parenting life.

"I don't like you right now, Daddy. You're a giant meanie and you're hurting my feelings."

"Yeah, well get in line, Holly. You're not the only one who doesn't like me. Now go. I need a minute to calm down."

Holly grunts and stomps her way down the hall. Her door slams, causing me to jump. I lean back against the couch and close my eyes. I know I'm dreaming when I think I can smell Delaney's perfume on my sofa. There's no way. She wasn't here long enough to leave a lingering scent like this.

Weeks ago, my life made sense, even if were messy and painful, and then Delaney comes to town and she's everywhere, including my dreams. Even if I wanted to, I wouldn't be able to stop thinking about her because in a matter of special moments, she's integrated herself into my life. I have no idea how to tell Holly that her newfound friend is going to leave and the only way to see her will be at the movies or on television.

After an hour or so, I finally relent and start to get dressed. All police officers are required to go. Our chief always asks another town to provide coverage for a few hours so everyone can attend. According to him, it's a good thing for the community to see all officers together.

I knock on Holly's door, but she tells me to go away. I get it, she's upset with me, but I'm not the bad guy. I wish she could see things my way or see the bigger picture. If it were so easy to be with Delaney, I'd jump at the opportunity. Besides, I'm certain I've missed my chance with her.

The kitchen door opens and my sister walks in. She comes down the hall, looking at me oddly. "She's boycotting the party," I tell her.

"Why?" Meredith asks.

"Because Delaney isn't here to do her hair."

The hall may be dim, but I can easily see my sister roll her eyes. "What?"

Meredith shakes her head. "Nothing."

"Clearly it's something."

My sister motions for me to follow her into my room. I do, and she shuts the door behind me. "My something is, you should've never gotten involved with Delaney Du Luca to begin with."

"We're not involved."

"You are. You let her into your home and into Holly's life. Everyone knows you waited to be the last one to buy her meet and greet tickets at the start of the festival. The whole town has seen you together, acting like a family.

Honestly, it's a bit ridiculous when you know she's not going to give up her career for you, let alone... "

"Let alone, what? The fact that I'm a single dad or drowning in debt? Which one of these is going to turn Delaney off the most?"

Meredith reaches for me, but I step away. "I didn't mean for it to sound so horrible. All I'm saying is, you should've protected Holly better. Delaney is going to leave and it'll likely be ten years before we ever see her again. Honestly, she's done nothing but interrupt lives."

I shake my head, unwilling to continue this conversation with my sister. "If you're going to do Holly's hair, she's in her room pouting. Delaney put her hair in some elaborate braid the other day, she really liked it." I leave my sister standing in my room while I head out of the house. I know she means well, but I'm an adult and should be able to make my own decisions without people judging me.

Every few seconds I'm checking my phone. I tell myself it's to see the time, but truthfully I'm hoping to find a text message from Laney. It's stupid, I know. When Holly finally emerges, she's dressed in her red Christmas dress my mom bought her and her hair is in curls. One quick glance at my sister tells me all I need to know. She did whatever she wanted and didn't take Holly's needs into consideration.

"You ready, punky?"

"Sure."

I lift her into the truck without another word to my sister. "You look very pretty," I tell Holly as I back out of the driveway. "I think Santa is going to think you're the prettiest girl in the room."

"Will Delaney be there?"

"I don't know, Holly. I think maybe she will because her

dad is the mayor, but Delaney is really busy sometimes."

"But she promised." Holly's head rests against the window, seemingly dejected. Maybe my sister's right, and I should've put a stop to the interactions between Holly and Delaney, but to see them together... I don't know, for one brief moment, Holly was happy. She was laughing and she hadn't done that in a while. I have Delaney to thank for bringing some cheer to my daughter's life, even if it's short lived.

The parking lot at the lodge is full, forcing me to park on the street. Holly and I walk hand in hand up the stairs and into the entryway, where the chief and his wife greet us. "Oh Holly, you're absolutely beautiful. Are you ready to see Santa?" Mrs. Floyd crouches down and tugs the ruffle on Holly's dress. She leans into me, acting bashful.

"It's good to see you, Mrs. Floyd. Chief." He nods as Holly and I pass by. Inside, the decorations are vast. The large tree in the center of the room sits in front of a giant red chair. Presents are stacked all around, each one with a child's name on it. This has been a town tradition for as long as I can remember. My parents used to bring Meredith and I here when we were younger.

Holly and I find our seats, which happen to be next to Shelby and Shawna. Shelby clutches my arm when she sees me and leans in. She goes to kiss me on the cheek and I hug her, creating an awkward situation.

"The perfect couple," my sister says as she greets us both. Internally, I groan and disengage as quickly as I can. I make sure to sit on the other side of Holly, putting at least two people between us. I'd like to sit my sister down and ask her why she's pushing for a relationship between Shelby and me. It's not like I've told her anything or shown I'm overly interested. I understand my sister wanting me to be happy, but she has to let me find my own path and do what's right for Holly, and I'm not sure Shelby is.

Volunteers from the high school gather all the kids and have them compete in games. Unfortunately, with Holly gone, it leaves me vulnerable to Shelby. She takes the seat next to me and in her not so subtle way, brushes her leg up against mine.

"I was thinking that it might be nice for you and Holly to come over on Christmas Eve."

"I'm not sure, Shelby. I'll need to check with my parents. We usually spend some time over there."

"Your sister says they don't have anything going on."

I look at her, studying her deeply. She's beaming and looks happy. Life would make sense with a partner, but I'm not there yet. Movement behind me catches my eye, I turn and find Delaney standing there. She watches me for a minute before smiling and walking away. I get up to chase her, to demand she speak to me, but my chief cuts me off.

"Fisher, I need you."

"But, Chief." Delaney disappears into the crowd. I strain to look for Calvin, but he too seems invisible.

"No buts. Come on, our Santa called out sick and I need you to fill in." The chief pushes me toward the back room, all while I'm still trying to find Laney.

"What?" I stop dead in my tracks. "You've got to be kidding me."

"I wish I were, but the suit makes me break out in hives and we can't let the children down."

"But... but..."

"Take one for the team, Fisher." He pushes me into the dressing room where Mrs. Claus is, dressed and ready to go. The door shuts behind me, leaving me trapped with no choice but to become the jolly fellow.

TWENTY-SEVEN

DELANEY

*A*ttending the policeman's dinner was the last thing I wanted to do; yet, because my father's the mayor, he asked that all his family be here. I couldn't really deny my dad, especially since this is the first time I've been home in ages and he's so proud of Dominic and me for doing what we love.

What I didn't count on, was seeing Aiden the second I walked in the door. Of course, he was with Shelby, sharing a table with her and her daughter. It took everything in me not to run up to Holly and pull her into my arms, to tell her how much I'm going to miss her. Instead, I stepped behind Calvin and hid so I wouldn't have to face her. Tomorrow's going to be hard enough as it is, knowing she'll never fully be a part of my life.

It's been days since I texted Aiden with my thoughts. I fully expected him to say something, either via phone or in person, but he's dodged me every chance possible. At first, I thought there was something wrong with my phone or it was the poor connection we have in the state, but everyone else could reach me. Then, the gossip started. Everywhere I went people gushed about the happy couple. Mindy told me not to listen, but it was hard to ignore.

Still is. I've never been one to be quick on the uptake, as demonstrated by the fact I never figured out Trey was cheating on me, but Aiden's message is loud and clear. He's chosen Shelby, and honestly, he's made the right choice for him and Holly, even if I'm hurt over it. Shelby's better for the both of them, despite how I'm feeling.

Once I get back to work, I'll forget these past couple of weeks and everything in my life will be crazy and hectic. My heart won't have time to long for a night without power where the three of us are cuddled on the couch together, or we're walking hand in hand down the street, stopping to look at the store displays, and it'll forget the snow angels. I'm not sure I'll ever be able to make one again without thinking about the Fishers.

My father notices my sullen expression and frowns. He pulls me into his arms and kisses the top of my head. I know he's not going to ask me what's wrong. He's always been so observant when it comes to my brother and me, we were never able to get away with anything when it came to him. Our mom, on the other hand, she was clueless or at least pretended to be.

"Delaney!" Holly yelling my name shakes me from my funk. I welcome her into my arms, hugging her as tightly as I can without breaking her or setting off her fight and flight response.

"You look so beautiful."

"Thank you. I thought you were coming over to do my hair."

I rack my brain, going over any of the conversations we've had and can't recall where I told her I'd come over and fix her hair. "You did? Why did you think that?"

She shrugs. "Because I thought you liked me."

I've never felt my heart break this much. I have to take a deep breath before I speak out of fear my voice is going to crack. I touch my nose to hers and smile before pulling back to look at her. "I do like you, Holly, so so very much. If you knew you wanted me to do your hair, all you had to do was call me."

"I don't have your number." Her hands go up, as if it's as simple as that.

"I'll give it to you, if you promise me one thing."

"What's that?"

"You call me, whenever you want to talk."

Holly's expression changes from glee to sadness. "Are you leaving soon?"

I nod, and fight back a wave of tears threatening to come forward. "I have to go back to work."

She doesn't say anything, but does rest her head on my shoulder and stays there with me while we watch the children go sit on Santa's lap. I'm surprised I haven't seen Aiden. Maybe he knows Holly and I need these last few moments together and is granting me this Christmas wish.

Soon it's Holly's turn to sit on Santa's lap, and she returns with her present, ripping open the paper to unveil a new doll. "I'm going to name her Laney," she says.

My mom reaches across the table and sets her hand down over Holly's. "What a beautiful name for a baby doll."

"Do you like it?" Holly turns to me.

I nod. "I love it." Watching Holly with her new toy makes me excited for when she opens all her gifts on Christmas morning. Thankfully, my brother doesn't mind helping me out and has promised to have all Aiden and Holly's Christmas gifts delivered and set under their tree tomorrow while we're at the festival play. Dominic swore he has a key to Aiden's and won't do anything illegal. I'm not sure I trust him, but I want everything to be a surprise for them.

When the last child has gone up, Dominic rushes up to Santa. "Oh dear, what is he doing?" my mom asks. She covers her face as her grown son sits on Santa's lap.

"What does Dominic want for Christmas this year?" Santa yells.

"Well Santa, I've been really good this year and there's only one thing I want."

"And what's that?"

"For Eileen Barnett to be my wife!"

There's a collective gasp among the entire room and all eyes are on Eileen, waiting for her reaction.

"Eileen?" Dom's voice has me turned to watch him. He's down on one knee with a box in his hand, waiting for his bride to be to come to him. My mom had said something about him asking her, but I figured he'd wait until Christmas to do it.

"Dominic, what are you doing?"

He clears his throat and holds the ring up higher. "Eileen Barnett, will you do me the honor of becoming my wife?"

Eileen covers her mouth and nods vigorously. "Yes. Yes I will." The entire lodge erupts in applause and my parents, along with Eileen's go over to greet the happy couple. I do what feels natural and pull Holly close, knowing that the next time I come to visit, she'll have a new mother and her father will be happy.

"Delaney Du Luca?" Santa yells my name. Holly looks and smiles.

"Santa wants you," she says, crawling off my lap. Ever so slowly, I get up, wondering what my parents have done.

Don't they know I'm more than capable of sharing the spotlight with my brother?

"Ho ho ho," Santa says as I sit down on his lap. I can honestly say I haven't done this in years, so many years. "And what would Delaney like for Christmas this year?"

"Oh Santa, I have everything I want."

Lies.

"Surely there's something you want?" his voice is a bit quieter this time and I figure, what do I have to lose?

"I wish Aiden had chosen me, Santa." Without waiting for his response, I leave his lap and return to my family. My mom shoots me a look and I shrug, not willing to share what I've told some man dressed up in a red suit. Chances are, I'll never see whoever is under the fake white beard again, so I'm not worried about any rumors being spread.

As the dinner winds down, my mom invites everyone back to our house to celebrate the engagement of Dominic and Eileen. Calvin and I leave early, to stop at the store and buy everything we can, just in case everyone takes my mom up on her offer.

By the time we arrive at my parents', cars line the street. "Does she do this often?" Calvin asks as he maneuvers the SUV into a tight spot in the driveway.

"I think Mom looks for any excuse to have a party or to have people over. Announcing it at the dinner makes it seem like no one is left out."

"You know this would never happen in California," Calvin states.

"I know. Ramona Falls is different. Vermont is different. The mayors are normal every day citizens who still live in their own houses and drive their own cars."

Calvin carries most of the groceries in with my dad there to help. The house is bustling with people and I find myself looking for Aiden, even though I know he wouldn't bring Holly over. The one time he was here, it's because I suggested it to his daughter, which left him no choice.

Once everything's unloaded and set out, I excuse myself, leaving Dominic and Eileen to shine in the spotlight.

"Ms. Du Luca, there are so many people out there; what if I forget my lines?"

"You won't, Betsy. You've been practicing every day for weeks and you haven't forgotten a single line or cue. You've got this." I set my arms around Betsy and pull her away from the curtain. The butterflies in my stomach are going crazy. I don't remember a time when I've been so nervous before, but I am. I want this play to go off without a hitch and I'm afraid something will go wrong.

The younger kids file in and take their places on the risers. When I see Holly, I wave and she beckons me over.

"My daddy wants to talk to you." She points behind me. I turn to find Aiden at the bottom of the stairs, fidgeting. Quickly, I look at Holly.

"Oh? About what?"

She shrugs. "He asked me to come get you."

"Okay," I tell her. "Go take your spot."

I stand tall and take each step confidently toward Aiden. I'm a trained actress and it's not going to matter what he tells me, I'll stay strong and stoic. Nothing emotional. I'll save the tears for later.

"Holly said you needed to speak with me."

Aiden nods and picks at his lower lip. I want to push his hand away, but instead clasp mine together.

"Aiden?"

"Right. Um... the rumors you hear; nothing's true. Shelby and I, we're not dating or anything. Our girls play together and she invites us over for dinner."

"Okay." Honestly, this is a relief, but why is he telling me now?

"And I wanted you to know... I mean ask you if you think I, I mean we, Holly and I fit into your life?"

I swallow hard and feel my eyes bug out. Aiden steps closer. "What I'm saying, Laney, is the Fishers would like a chance to be in your life."

My head begins to spin and my palms start to sweat. Behind me my name is called and Aiden is looking at me, waiting for an answer... an answer to whether he and Holly fit into my life. I smile, from ear to ear, and nod.

"Delaney, we need to start now," Mrs. Winters scolds.

"Can we talk about this after the show?"

Aiden nods. "My parents are taking Holly to their house. Do you want to come over?"

I do. So much. "I'll be there." I'm tempted to kiss him, but not here. This makeshift backstage doesn't provide for much privacy and I don't know what he's said to Holly about me... us.

I rush back up the stairs with a whole new outlook on tonight. This show is going to be amazing. My lead actor and actress come forward, prepped and ready to go. "This is it; all the hard work comes down to this moment. If you mess up, keep going. This is a live production and we can't stop. Okay?" They both nod, but look completely scared. "I'll be right over there if you need me, but I'm confident you won't."

"Thank you, Ms. Du Luca," Betsy says. She takes a deep breath, but her co-star doesn't. He stares off into space, either thinking he's the best or fighting the nerves rolling in his stomach.

As soon as I step off to the side, the curtain goes up and the spotlight hits center stage. Mrs. Winters directs the choir to start their song while the older kids get into place. As soon as Betsy says her first line, the anxiety I've felt all day lifts. It could be because Aiden is sitting in the front row, beaming at his daughter.

TWENTY-EIGHT

AIDEN

I have an immense amount of pride after watching Holly sing her heart out. I may be biased, but she was the best one out of her class. The play wasn't half bad either, from what I caught of it. I focused solely on Holly to actually watch the performance. However, by the way everyone is clapping around me, I can easily say the festival play is a success.

Mrs. Winters and Delaney take center stage after the actors take their curtain call. I can't take my eyes off Delaney, knowing I have so much to tell her. If it weren't for Dominic, I don't think I'd be ready to lay my heart on the line.

"Hey, man, thanks for your help tonight. The proposal couldn't have gone any better." Eileen gives me a hug after Dominic pats me on the shoulder. *I want to ask him where his sister went, but know I need to tell him how I feel so he doesn't butt in like he did last time.*

"You're welcome. Listen, I need to talk to you, Dom."

"Sounds serious."

"It is. Do you think we can go out back?" I motion toward the door and he nods. Dom kisses Eileen, who tells me she'll make sure to stay with Holly.

Holly, who glued herself to Delaney's side, making it near impossible for me to focus on the task tonight. I wanted to pull out my phone and snap picture after picture of the two of them together so I have something to look at when Delaney's back in California.

Dominic follows me into the back room, shutting the door behind him. "Is this about you calling Delaney up to sit on your lap? I gotta say, Fisher, that was a bit creepy."

"My note said she was next. I was following the list."

"Right, okay. So what do you want to talk about?"

"Well... your sister, actually."

"What about her?"

"I think I'm falling in love with her?"

"Is that so?"

I nod and start pacing the room. "Ever since I pulled her over, I haven't been able to get her out of my mind. It didn't matter where I went, she was there, like this beacon begging me to follow."

"So follow her," Dominic says as if it's so easy.

"What if I can't exist in her world?"

"Then she'll exist in yours. Listen, Fisher, I may joke around a lot and may have teased you about my sister, but I have never seen her look at someone the way she looks at you. She's ridiculously smitten and makes gaga eyes anytime your name is brought up."

"But she lives in California."

Dominic nods. "She does, but she can live anywhere and so can you. Thing is, love is supposed to bridge gaps and all that. Just try it and see how things go."

"It's a risk. Holly is already attached."

Dominic comes closer, putting his hand on my shoulder. "Waking up, driving, taking a shower – all risks we're willing to take each and every day. If you don't jump, you'll second-guess your decision for the rest of your life."

"You're right," I say with relief.

"Of course I am, but wait... I thought you and Shelby—"

I shake my head. "No, only friends, but I haven't done a very good job relaying my feelings to her. I will though, for everyone's sake."

"Do me a favor, Fisher."

"What's that?"

"Don't hurt her." Dominic doesn't wait for me to respond before he opens the door and leaves. I follow behind, intent on finding Holly so we can leave, only to run right into Shelby. I suppose now is as good a time as ever.

"We need to talk, Shelby."

"Oh?" Her eyes light up and instantly I feel like a cad.

"Look, our girls get along really well, but you and I can't be anything more than friends."

"Oh... I wasn't expecting you to say that."

"I know, I just—"

"You're in love with Delaney. Everyone knows it, I had just hoped I was more your speed."

"You probably would be, if things were different."

Shelby steps forward and kisses me on the cheek. "Have a merry Christmas, Aiden. I hope you find what you're looking for."

I think I have found what I'm looking for. She's currently holding my daughter's hand and whispering something in her ear. I want to be in on their secret, holding both of their hands, sharing their laughter and smiles.

Telling Delaney how I feel is the right thing to do. Figuring out how we're going to make it work though, well, that's a whole other challenge. Thankfully, we still have until after New Year's Day before we're faced with her leaving.

Along with my parents, we meet Holly as she comes off the stage. She jumps into my arms, and I twirl her around, much to her delight. I set her down with her black patent leather boots resting on the packed snow. "You were amazing."

"You couldn't hear me, Daddy." She laughs and sways from side to side, holding the hem of her dress so people around her can see the ruffles.

"I could hear you, punky. You were the best one up there. Are you ready to go to Grandma and Grandpa's?"

"Yes, for a sleepover!" Holly jumps up and down until my father wraps her in his arms as he tries to wrestle her coat on. Each year the fire department provides the production with heaters so the actors and singers can wear their holiday best without anyone freezing.

I crouch down and give Holly a kiss on her cheek. "I'll see you tomorrow at church."

Holly cups my face between her hands and runs her nose against mine. "Okay, Daddy. I love you."

Not as half as much as I love you, but those words fail me as my throat swells. This child of mine has no idea what she means to me. "I love you more, punky."

"Come on, Holly; I believe Grandma made brownies for dinner," my dad says, earning a loud cheer from Holly. Mom smacks my dad on the arm, scolding him.

"They're for dessert and you know it." My parents walk off, with my father carrying Holly. Delaney is still on stage, assisting with the tear down. I want to be suave and rush up the stairs so I can pick her up, but I'm far too reserved to do something like that. Besides, we haven't talked yet and we need to. I'm willing to do whatever it takes to give it a go between us.

My lingering finally catches Delaney's eye. She waves and motions for me to meet her on the side where the stairs are. "I'm going to be another hour or so, depending on how fast the volunteers work. I don't want to leave Mrs. Winters with all of it."

"Do you want my help?"

Delaney shakes her head. "No, go on home and relax. I'll meet you there as soon as I'm done." She smiles and the glint in her eye has me curious about how things will be later. I lean in and kiss her forehead, desperately wanting to kiss her lips, but this isn't the time or place.

I'm feeling euphoric on my drive home. I take each road slowly, watching for black ice and so I can admire the decorations. I need to get out and put some up for Holly since she's been asking me. It's something I'll do tomorrow morning before I meet her and my parents at church. It'll be a nice surprise for her.

The high I'm feeling quickly dissipates when I pull into my driveway. The lights I only just thought about hanging, are hung and twinkling in the night sky. My tree is lit, which I know I didn't have on when I left.

Carefully, I enter my house, calling out to see if anyone is there. It's times like this I wish I kept a gun hidden in my garage so I can arm and protect myself from the unknown.

I turn the corner, into the living room, and my mouth drops open. My tree, the one I left unlit and completely void of presents, is sparkling brightly and presents fill the floor, leaving barely any walking space. Cautiously, I bend down and pick one up, it's to Holly, and so is the next one, the next and the one after that. In fact, most belong to her with a few for me mixed in. There's only one explanation and I don't want to believe Delaney would do something like this.

In the kitchen, I pull open the refrigerator to grab a beer, only my somewhat barren shelves are fully stocked. The results are the same when I open the cupboards. There's food stocked in tightly, every variety you can think of. I don't know if it's anger I feel or my pride slipping away. There's a sting from the proverbial slap across my face, shaming me for not providing for my daughter. "Son of a—"

The side door opens, cutting my words off. The woman, who not hours ago, I told I wanted try to have a relationship with, is standing there with a confused expression on her face. Maybe I'm wrong to assume she did this, but there isn't anyone else who would. People know I struggle, but I always manage to feed my kid. Holly doesn't go hungry.

"Something wrong?" Delaney asks.

I can feel the tick in my jaw become stronger as I try to control my temper. The last thing I want to do is lash out at her, but I'm on the cusp of yelling. "Do you have anything to do with any of this?"

Delaney looks in the living room, and then at me. She doesn't even have to tell me because I can see the guilt written all over her face.

"Why would you do this? How did you do this?"

"Dominic has a key."

"Great, that reminds me I need to get that back from him, but that doesn't answer my first question. Why?"

"I don't understand why you're not happy."

"Are you serious right now? In a matter of seconds you proved to me, before we even started dating, the reason why we can't."

"Fish…"

"No. You can't sweet talk me into thinking this is okay when it's not. Look at this, Delaney. There are enough presents for each kid in Holly's class to have two from you. What kind of message are you trying to send?"

"I just wanted you guys to have a good Christmas."

"And what happens next year or the year after that when you're not around? Huh? Then what? Who is going to make sure each Christmas is the same? It's not going to be me. You've already shown me that the stuff I bought her isn't enough. So you what, decided to quadruple my efforts?"

"It wasn't like that."

"Then what was it like?"

"I don't know. I saw the stuff and I bought it. It's simple as that."

I nod, hating the fact that I'm about to ruin Holly's Christmas. "I think I made a mistake earlier, asking you to come over."

"Aiden?"

I shake my head. "I can't be in a relationship where I'm not an equal, where my daughter thinks she'll get whatever she wants because of who you are. This… saying it's too much doesn't even cover it. You went overboard. You violated the trust I have in your brother and you made me feel like a charity case."

"Aiden, you have to believe me, that wasn't my intention at all. I only wanted you and Holly to be comfortable. I could do that for you."

I look at Delaney, who has tears falling down her face. "That's just it. You can do that for me, but I can't even do this for my own daughter. I was foolish to think I could look past your career and have a normal relationship with you. There will never be anything normal when it comes to you."

"Aiden, please don't."

"I'm sorry, Delaney. I really am."

She nods and heads toward the door. She pauses with it open, likely waiting for me to ask her to stay, but I won't. I can't.

TWENTY-NINE

DELANEY

New York City disappears from sight as soon as we hit cloud coverage. Calvin is sleeping next to me, having passed out the moment he sat down in his first class seat. Being at the airport for a six am flight meant we left Ramona Falls at midnight for the four hour drive, upsetting my parents, but they understood when I told them I had to go back for an early morning schedule of reshoots. The lie fell easily, but there was no way I could tell my family how humiliated I felt after what I did for Aiden and Holly. I thought I was doing the right thing, but after listening to him and seeing the anguish I caused, I knew it was wrong. As much as I would've loved to stay and celebrate Christmas with my family, the thought of being there, where I almost had everything and let it slip through my fingers, doesn't seem like the best place for me.

I close my eyes and rest my head against the cold airplane window. It does nothing to soothe the pounding in my head gained from the hours of crying. I feel horrible for Calvin, having to sit there and listen to me cry. I have no doubt the sniffling annoyed him after a while, yet he'd never say anything to affirm that. Sometimes, I hate that he works for me because I really need someone like him to put me in my place.

I jostle awake as the plane touches down at LAX. Looking over at Calvin, he's reading the paper and looking haggard. "You can have the rest of the month off," I tell him.

"Thanks."

He says nothing else, leading me to believe he's upset with me, as he should be. From what I gathered, he was having a great time in Ramona and I ruined it by meddling in affairs I shouldn't. In fact, I should've steered clear of Aiden and his daughter, and admired from the outside, but I couldn't. Selfishly, I had to be the center of their attention and in the process, I fell hard and ruined everything.

Calvin leads the way through the airport. My head is down and my long auburn hair stays hidden under a beanie. Still, I don't go unnoticed. People say my name; they whisper it, wondering if it's me they see or someone else. I do everything I can to keep my expression stoic even though I'm on the verge of a meltdown. It can't happen here, not in public. Celebrities aren't allowed to show emotion. It has to be saved for the privacy of your home; that is when I'll break down, inside the walls of my empty home where no one can hear me. It's there, in the quiet, where the tears will flow and my heart will burst open with pain, and I have no one to blame but myself.

Calvin gathers our luggage and looks for the driver he scheduled before we left Vermont. He does all the talking, proving to whoever is watching, that I'm nothing but a diva. As much as I want to argue the point, there's no use. I let my status and checkbook think for me and now I'm paying the price.

Holly is as well. I hate I didn't find her to say goodbye,

to tell her how wonderful I think she is, and how I'll always think about her. With any luck, Aiden will fix things between him and Shelby and give his daughter the mother she needs. I have no doubt Shelby will be an excellent partner and mother for them.

The drive to my house is much like the flight. I stare out the window, wishing I were anywhere but here. "I should've gone somewhere else."

"You still have reshoots the day after Christmas, Delaney."

Right, work. It's never ending and while it used to bother me — filming back-to-back movies — I'll take it now so my mind can focus on anything except Ramona Falls. The quicker I forget, the faster I'll be able to move on.

Calvin carries my luggage into my quiet, cold and life-less condo. Even with all the gizmos and gadgets keeping my lights on, you can feel the lack of love in here.

"I'll see you next week," he says, not letting me forget I've given him the week off. I nod and give him a hug.

"Merry Christmas, Calvin."

"Merry Christmas, Delaney."

Once the door clicks shut, I let the tears flow. I didn't cry when Trey cheated on me, at least not like this. The pain I feel is like nothing ever before, and think it only took me seconds to fall in love with Aiden. I was stupid to think things between us would work or even be easy, but I never thought he'd reject me over a few gifts.

"Oh, who are you kidding, Delaney. A few means two or three, not a hundred." The words I mutter aloud only add to the burning in my chest. I should've been more cautious. I should've put myself in Aiden's shoes, and maybe checked with him first to see if he was okay with me buying things for Holly, but I never considered how he'd feel or what he'd think. I only thought about Holly and how happy she'd be on Christmas.

I drag my luggage upstairs and start to unpack. My newly bought winter wardrobe won't serve me much here, but I'm not ready to give the clothes away. I find an empty tote to store most of the clothes in, but keep out the scarves and hats, knowing I can wear them here and create a fashion statement. All it takes is for one photo to cause a stir and increase sales. Right now, it's the least I can do for the people back home.

My phone rings with Mindy's name showing on the screen. I send her to voicemail, not ready to tell her what I've done. There's no doubt word has spread that I'm gone. However, leaving without saying goodbye to the people I love is right up on the list of worst things I've done. It was late and I just wanted to get out of town and be on the first flight back home.

Home. This is my home. As much as I wanted to call Ramona Falls my home, I can't. I'm Hollywood through and through, made evident by my actions.

I<small>T</small>'s two days before Christmas and the park is bustling full of children. They laugh, play and sing carols. Each one of them reminds me of Holly. I miss her. I miss her infectious smile, her blue eyes and untamable spirit. I shouldn't be here, not without a child of my own to bring, yet I can't stay away. It's like I need to see the happiness these children have in order to make my pain cease for a small moment in time.

I've kept my phone off, unwilling to talk to anyone from home, including my mother, and stopped myself from calling Calvin to beg him to come over and watch sappy movies with me. The man has a life away from me and I need to respect that, even though he'd drop whatever he was doing and come to my rescue because he's paid to do so.

The other reason my phone is off is so I don't want to look on social media sites for pictures of Aiden and Shelby. I would suspect she's consoling him over my deceit. It's something I would do if I were interested in a man. I'm sure she was there at sunrise with a coffee in her hand, offering him a listening ear, although his kitchen is fully stocked and should last him at least a month, if not longer.

I wish I could go back and do things differently. I don't know if I'd let myself fall so easily for Aiden and Holly. I'd likely keep my guard up and stay at my parents' more, be a homebody instead of putting myself in places where I knew I'd likely run into Aiden. I definitely wouldn't have done the play. The only reason I did was because Aiden suggested I take a leap of faith. Deep down, I felt like I had something to prove to him, to show him I'm more than an actress making a living on the big screen. In the end, I proved nothing.

Honestly, he had no chance once I set my sights on him. What does that make me? I'm not sure a word has been invented for what I've done because overbearing nut job doesn't really cut it. I used my brother, telling him that this would be a good thing for the Fishers and he bought it, betraying his best friend.

I've likely ruined lifelong friendships because of how selfish I am. I'm going to have to make it up to Dominic. Maybe I'll pay for his and Eileen's honeymoon or destination wedding because going back to Ramona Falls anytime soon doesn't appeal to me.

A little girl cries out, having fallen and it looks like she's scraped her knee. I rush over to her, only to stop when her mother or nanny arrives first. I look around, wondering if anyone is staring or gabbing about the odd woman who is trying to intervene.

"What is wrong with me?" I mutter to myself, hoping someone or something will give me an answer. I look around, but the other men and women in the park keep their attention on their children. I shouldn't be here. This park isn't the place for a single woman mending a broken heart.

THIRTY

The banging on my door continues. It's coupled with Dominic yelling my name. Clearly, he knows I'm home and it should be evident I'm ignoring him. He's not getting the picture. I want to be left alone, and the last person I want to talk to is him. He asked me not to hurt his sister; I did exactly that, not twenty-four hours later. It wasn't my intention, but Delaney overstepped and I lost my temper. Actually, I kept the rage I was feeling in check, but my words were harsh and I made her cry. Something I never thought I'd do. She's been so nice and accommodating, letting Holly hang all over her. Delaney didn't have to be like that, and yet she gave so selflessly. Too much if you're looking at the floor under our Christmas tree full of presents.

I lift my beer bottle to my lips and tilt my head back, waiting for a trickle or drop to tease the back of my throat. Over the last ten or so hours I've done nothing but sit on the couch and stare at the tree. The six-pack of bottles, courtesy of Delaney, sits empty at my feet. Well, five do since the last one is still in my hand.

Our tree is beautiful. Not because it's something my daughter decorated. It's because there's a story behind it. Delaney did that. She gave Holly a story to tell friends, something to remember each time we go to Mr. Steve's for a tree in years to come. The fact that Delaney came over and helped decorate it, well, that just adds to the beauty, and I destroyed it all.

I'm sure there was another way for Delaney and me to discuss what happened. I could've easily asked her to take the presents back, to donate them to the shelter or a child's home for kids who need a little Christmas magic in their lives. Holly has some presents, and while I may not be able to buy her the best of everything, my parents are there to make sure she has plenty. What Delaney did was take gift giving and put it on steroids.

The banging finally stops. The quiet is peaceful. I close my eyes, but see images of Delaney crying and I can't stand to look at the pain I caused her.

My eyes fly open when my door slams shut. "What the—"

"Mind telling me what's going on?"

I hold up my empty bottle of beer and shake it. Dominic shakes his head. I can see the disappointment in his eyes. Its different from the look he gave me after Heather died. Then, he sat with me so I wouldn't hurt myself or do something stupid.

Somehow, I have a feeling he's not here to be my support. "There's more in the fridge if you want one."

"It's eight in the morning, Fisher. Beer is the last thing either of us need."

"Yeah well, I stopped keeping track of time about ten or is it twelve, hours now?"

Dominic stands in front of me with his shoulders

square. "The one thing I asked you to do is not hurt her, and what do you do?"

"Hurt her," I tell him.

"Do you know what it's like to get a phone call from my mother crying hysterically because her Christmas is ruined?"

"Delaney go overboard on her presents too?"

Dominic sighs angrily before answering. "No, she left."

I sit up straight, and wobble slightly. "What?"

"Last night around midnight, she and Calvin left. They had a six am flight out of New York. Apparently, she has to work, but I knew something else had to be up and by the look of things here, I'm right. So what I need you to do is sober up quickly and tell me what's going on."

Dominic doesn't give me a chance to respond before he disappears into my kitchen. The sound of water running and the cupboards opening and closing lead me to believe he's making a pot of coffee. At this rate though, I may need two.

I'm able to make it down to the bathroom, but not without bumping into the wall a few times. I refuse to look at myself in the mirror, already hating the way I feel. I splash cold water on my face, shivering as droplets go down my neck and into my shirt.

Dominic is there, in the doorway, with a mug of steaming coffee. He hands it to me and I drink, gagging at the strong taste. "This is nasty."

Dom shrugs. "Can't say I really care right now." No, I suppose he doesn't. Honestly, I'm not sure if telling Dominic about the argument Delaney and I had will make a difference. I'm also not sure I believe him when he says she has to work. Delaney was looking forward to spending

Christmas with her parents, I'm sure she would've pushed work off as long as possible.

"Ready to talk?"

I nod and motion toward the living room. He follows me there and takes a seat in the chair while I sit on the sofa. "I came home to this last night."

"And?" he asks, without looking at the pile of presents on the floor.

"And... it's excessive. It's overstepping. It's showing my daughter that Delaney can buy her anything she wants and I can't."

Finally, Dominic looks at the mess around the tree, but he doesn't say anything. He picks up a few presents, examines them, and sets them back into place.

"Let me guess. You freaked out and thought she was trying to buy your love?"

"Actually, that never crossed my mind, but I did freak out."

"Why?" he asks.

"Because I can't give Delaney the type of relationship she's looking for or needs. I'm a police officer for crying out loud. I make barely enough to feed my kid and pay my mortgage. How am I supposed to keep up with Delaney?"

"Have you ever thought that maybe you don't need to keep up with her? That you just need to be you, the man she's in love with from Ramona Falls? Be the man she trusts with her secrets, desires and be there when she comes home from a hectic day at work to hold her and tell her that tomorrow will be better?

"Delaney's life isn't about money, and I can guarantee you she did this because she wants you and Holly to have the best freaking Christmas ever."

"It's too much."

"No, you know what's too much? Delaney paying off my parents' mortgage so my mom can retire, or her paying off every bill they have so our dad can take our mom on the vacation she's always dreamed of. Or Delaney getting us box and ice seats because she wanted to do something nice for you."

"That was for Calvin," I remind him.

Dominic shakes his head. "Do you think if it were for Calvin, you would've been invited? Think about it, Fisher. You were the only non-Du Luca there. That trip was for you."

It takes me a minute to find my words. "Just proves my point. I can't compete with her."

Dominic scoffs. "Delaney doesn't know any other way to show you she cares. Maybe you can teach her, but right now, in her life, people buy gifts for the ones they love. The only thing she meant here, is for you and Holly to have the best Christmas you've had since before Heather passed away. She's not trying to one up you or make you feel inadequate. She's trying to show you how much you mean to her."

Dominic sighs and then becomes silent. He's looking down at the ground, likely waiting for me to say something. Thing is, I don't know what to say. It'd be so easy to wash my hands of this and say oh well, but the truth of the matter is, I love her and have felt horrible since she left. I should've chased her and told her how sorry I am.

"What do I do to fix this?"

"Go to her," Dominic says, as if it's that easy. "Call Calvin and ask him... no, beg him to help you. He'll know what to do." Dominic pulls open his wallet and tosses his credit card at me. "Use it for airline tickets, rental car, every flower you can buy or whatever. I already added your name on there so you shouldn't have any problems."

"I can't use your card."

"You can and will." Dominic stands. "Fix this Fisher, because I really hate knowing my sister is hurting." Dominic leaves, slamming my door on his way out. It only takes me seconds to find Calvin's name and press the call button. The phone rings six times before going to voicemail. I call back, and back again until he finally picks up.

"You better be dying in a ditch somewhere because it's five in the morning and I'm on vacation."

"Oh."

"Oh is all you have to say? What do you want, Aiden?"

"I'm sorry to wake you. I didn't think about the time difference."

"Uh huh."

"Anyway, I really messed up with Delaney and I need to fix things."

Calvin groans. "I think it might be a little too late."

"I know, but I have to try. I've spoken to Dominic and he helped me see things through Delaney's eyes. I need to do something to make things right."

"What do you have in mind?"

"That's just it, I don't know," I tell him. "I've never really been super romantic and I have a feeling Delaney needs romance right now."

"Yeah she does, so listen and listen good."

Calvin spends the next hour giving me suggestions until I finally decide on what I'm going to do. The next hour is spent going over the plan and how he's going to help. The only thing I have to do is sober up so I can pick Holly up from my parents' and set the plan into motion.

When Calvin and I hang up, I spend however long it

takes moving the presents from Delaney into my room. If Holly is going to open them, I want Delaney to be here when she does. Delaney deserves to experience the Christmas joy that comes from having a little girl wake up and be surprised by what Santa brought her.

THIRTY-ONE

DELANEY

"*M*erry Christmas Eve," the hostess says as I walk past her to the table where my friend, Lana sits. She's wearing a wide brim hat, the kind you find on the beach, only we're in the middle of a restaurant.

"Who are you hiding from?" I ask as I sit down. She's the only call I've taken since I arrived back home, aside from my mother's. When Lana invited me out for lunch, I was tempted to tell her no because I don't feel like it, but staying home and wallowing isn't doing me any good either.

"The paps are everywhere," she mutters before picking up her drink. "I can't escape them."

I giggle, and keep my comments to myself. I met Lana when she had a three-scene part in one of my movies. We hit it off, sort of, and stayed in touch. Lana is everything but what she wants to be, an A-list celebrity.

"I think you're fine," I tell her even though I'm not sure, but I'm not worried and neither should she be. Besides, cameras aren't allowed in this restaurant.

"You never know." Lana removes her hat slowly and pulls a compact out of her oversized purse so she can fix her hair. "This one time I was at NoVu and they were everywhere. Their flashes kept blinding me. I couldn't see for days and when I could, I saw white lights. It was horrible." It takes everything in me to keep from rolling my eyes. To each their own, I guess. "Where's your delish bodyguard?" she asks.

I shake my head slightly. "On vacation, hopefully somewhere tropical."

"I may be in need of his services. My agent keeps telling me I'm getting the lead across from Denz, and well, you know how aggressive the paps are when he's around."

Denzel Washington? I want to scoff and call her out, but it's no use. Instead, I drink from my glass of water and study the menu while telling her Calvin isn't for hire.

"But surely, he freelances?"

"He doesn't. I mean he could, if he wanted to, but he works for me."

"And you're not interested in sharing?"

I shrug. "It'll depend on my shooting schedule. If I'm not doing anything, sure." It'll never happen in a million years. If Calvin knew I was out right now, he'd throw a fit.

The waiter comes by and takes our order. Once he's gone, Lana continues talking about her upcoming job where she'll play a private investigator hunting Denz. Why she doesn't call the man by his full name boggles my mind, but I let it go without saying anything.

"What's your next role?"

"Well, I have reshoots starting the day after Christmas and about mid-January I'll start working on a rom-com where I play a jilted bride."

"Oh, it's like true life imitating art."

I look at her oddly and she smiles. "I've never been left at the altar."

"Well close enough, when Trey ran off with his baby mama. I mean, it's probably a good thing because had you married him, he probably would've taken your money to give to her."

And this is why I should've stayed home. If I wasn't already depressed, I am now. Thanks, Lana. "Well, luckily for me, Trey made the right decision and... well, did whatever."

"Have you heard from him?"

I shake my head. "We have nothing to talk about. So tell me, what else is going on?" I ask quickly changing the subject.

"Oh nothing really," she says. "I go for auditions and sit by the phone. This role with Denz will really catapult my career. I'll be on your level and every part will land in my lap."

"I wish. I have to work for mine just as you do."

"Yeah..." she trails off and picks up her phone, which is a no-no in this restaurant. If she plans to make it in Hollywood, she might want to start by following the rules.

"You know, Lana. I just remembered I have to meet my agent. I completely forgot." I throw down a twenty for the food I'm not going to eat.

"But it's Christmas Eve."

"I know, she's such a slave driver." For the second time this week I make up an excuse about work to get out of a situation. Not my finest moments, that's for sure.

Outside, I slip on my hat and wrap my scarf around my neck. It's not cold, but a bit chilly, and I find myself missing the snow. I don't miss the wet though.

I pass through the park on my way home, the one with

all the decorations. The fake snow machine is pumping out flakes. I stand under it, hoping to catch one or two, but they flutter in every other direction.

I'd give anything to make a snow angel right now, to be with Holly, to be ice skating and holding her hand.

I pull out my phone to call Aiden, praying he'll let me speak with his daughter, only I can't bring myself to push the button to make his phone ring. I owe him an apology, but don't know if I have the right words to tell him how sorry I am. I never meant to make him feel like less of a man.

Instead of grabbing a cab, I decide to walk a bit longer. The decorations on these houses look nothing like the ones in Ramona Falls. The lack of snow makes the giant inflatable snowman and wooden Santa with his reindeer look out of place, but at least they're in the spirit. That's more than I can say for my house.

I finally call for a taxi once the sun goes down. The young man tells me about his daughter having her first Christmas, and how she's already trying to open the presents under the tree. I think he's hoping his story will make me smile, but all it does is make me miss Aiden and Holly more. Even my parents. I should've never left so hastily. When he pulls into my parking lot, I give him a large tip and wish him and his family a merry Christmas.

Inside, all my lights are off, which is odd since I have everything on a timer. I flip the switch as I walk into my living room and scream out, not only in fear, but in elation because standing there, in front of a fully decorated tree are Aiden and Holly.

"Surprise!" Holly yells as she comes barreling toward me. I catch her in my arms and we both fall to the ground. I'm unable to stop the tears from flowing.

"What're you doing here?" I ask her as I hold her face between my hands. I need my eyes to see that she's real.

"We came for Christmas?"

"I'm sorry what?"

Aiden clears his throat and offers me a hand to help me stand. When I go to pull my hand away, he tightens his grip. "I have something to say."

I nod, waiting for him to continue.

"I know your secret," he says. "The one you told Santa."

"How?"

Aiden smiles and steps closer. "Because I filled in that night. I was Santa. I called you up to sit on my lap so I could get an idea of what to buy you for Christmas and you told Santa... well me, that you wanted me to choose you. Thing is, I chose you the day I pulled you over, and I'm here to ask for your forgiveness. I acted like a fool and I wasn't thinking properly."

"No, Aiden, I shouldn't have done what I did." I refrain from blurting out that I bought all those presents in case he's tossed them out or given them away.

"True, but I overreacted, and I'm sorry. Please forgive me, but only after I tell you. Ever since Heather passed away, I've struggled to make ends meet. Men have pride when it comes to taking care of their families and when we can't, well let me just say, it weighs heavily on us. So to walk in and see everything you did for us, I took it hard when I should've talked to you first about it."

"I'm sorry I overstepped. I promise, it won't happen again."

"Do you forgive me?" he asks.

"Of course," I tell him. "Do you forgive me?"

He nods. "I do, Laney."

"Is it my turn?" Holly asks, jumping up and down.

"Yes, punky. It's your turn." Aiden pulls me farther into the living room where I can see the tree clearly.

"What's her name?"

"Her name is Merry," Holly says.

"Merry. I love it."

"Me too, but this isn't our surprise."

"It's not?" I look from her to Aiden. He shrugs even though I know he knows what's going on.

Holly grabs my hand and makes me stand in a certain spot. She then crawls under the tree and pulls out a box before situating herself on one knee.

"Holly?"

"Delaney, you're the bestest person I know and I was wondering if you'd be my bestest friend?" Holly holds up a black box. I take it and open it. Tears instantly cloud my vision. Nestled inside the black velvet is a friendship necklace with both our names on it.

"Oh Holly, I would love to be your bestest friend." I pull her into my arms and whisper into her ear, "I love you, sweet girl."

"I love you, too."

When she steps away, I gasp. Aiden is now on his knee with a box in his hand. "What're you doing?"

"Open it."

With a shaky hand, I push the lid open to find a beautiful gemstone ring. "Aiden?"

"It's not much, it's a start." He takes the ring and slips it on my finger. "This is my promise to you, Laney, to build a foundation for us to strive together as a couple and family. I promise to always see both sides of the coin, and when I don't, I'll ask you for an explanation. Most of all, I promise to be your Fish and Santa when you need me the most."

My hands cup his cheeks and I finally, after all these years, get to kiss this man knowing I never have to let him go, all while his daughter and my bestest friend cheers us on.

ACKNOWLEDGMENTS

What a blast I had writing this story. Living in Vermont, we have the Christmas feels all the time, so it was easy to combine many of the towns into Santa's Secret, anything from how they look, to their winter festivals, to the one large mall we have in the state. Yes, we only have one large mall. It's rather sad. Mostly, it was great to talk about my father-in-law's tree farm. Growing and selling Christmas trees has been his passion for as long as I've been in the family, and while I don't work at during the winter, I've been there plenty of times to see the inner workings. Mr. Steve, aka my father-in-law, also makes his own maple syrup and maple sugar. It's all very Vermonty.

Many thanks to Yvette & Briggs for helping me push through this story. I appreciate the guidance, long talks and the threats of coming to town to make me write. One day, I'm going to see if you follow through on those!

Lots of thanks to Ena & Amanda for organizing the cover reveal, Heidi Pharo for encouraging me to write this story, and Kellie Montgomery for dropping everything and editing because I missed so many deadlines. I blame my daughter for getting hurt and needing surgery... not really, but yeah.

Thank you for reading, sharing, talking, buying and the overall support. Not only with Santa's Secret, but my other work as well.

ABOUT THE AUTHOR

Heidi is a New York Times and USA Today Bestselling author.

Originally from the Pacific Northwest, she now lives in picturesque Vermont, with her husband and two daughters. Also renting space in their home is an over-hyper Beagle/Jack Russell, Buttercup and a Highland West/Mini Schnauzer, JiLL and her brother, Racicot.

When she's isn't writing one of the many stories planned for release, you'll find her sitting court-side during either daughter's basketball games.

Forever My Girl, is set to release in theaters on January 19, 2018, starring Alex Roe and Jessica Rothe.

Don't miss more books by Heidi McLaughlin! Sign up for her newsletter, follow her on Amazon, Book Bub or join the fun in her fan group!

Connect with Heidi!

www.heidimclaughlin.com
heidi@heidimclaughlin.com

ALSO BY HEIDI MCLAUGHLIN

THE BEAUMONT SERIES

Forever My Girl – Beaumont Series #1

My Everything – Beaumont Series #1.5

My Unexpected Forever – Beaumont Series #2

Finding My Forever – Beaumont Series #3

Finding My Way – Beaumont Series #4

12 Days of Forever – Beaumont Series #4.5

My Kind of Forever – Beaumont Series #5

Forever Our Boys - Beaumont Series #5.5

The Beaumont Boxed Set - #1

THE BEAUMONT SERIES: NEXT GENERATION

Holding Onto Forever

THE ARCHER BROTHERS

Here with Me

Choose Me

Save Me

LOST IN YOU SERIES

Lost in You

Lost in Us

THE BOYS OF SUMMER

Third Base

Home Run

Grand Slam

THE REALITY DUET

Blind Reality

Twisted Reality

SOCIETY X

Dark Room

Viewing Room

Play Room

STANDALONE NOVELS

Stripped Bare

Blow

Sexcation

SNEAK PEEK OF IT MUST'VE BEEN THE MISTLETOE

BY L.P. DOVER

"Be careful with the pictures," I warned.

My students carefully passed the century-old photos around the room. Some faces were lit with wonderment, while others couldn't care less—as was the case with most high school students.

I had always been fascinated with history. My grandfather had preserved the pictures as much as he could, by putting them into protective coverings. Each one was a piece of my heritage. Not many people could trace their family back as far as we could. Maybe that was why I had followed in my grandfather's footsteps and studied history in college.

Natalie, one of my most inquisitive students, held up the before and after picture of my house. Her chocolate-colored hair was pulled high into a ponytail and she had on a black and red Riverview High sweatshirt. "Is this the same place?"

I walked over and smiled. "It is. Over the years, my family upgraded and restored the original Hamilton Manor.

My grandparents left it to me in their will. When my grandfather died over the summer, it passed to me."

She gasped. "That's amazing. Well, not the part about your grandfather, but that you can actually walk in the same places your ancestors did all those years ago."

That was one of the things I loved about my house. "I couldn't agree more. My grandfather used to tell me stories about it when I was growing up. And I always dug around the yard, hoping to find something. Sometimes, I did—mainly old tools. Most of them were put in the history museum." We'd just wrapped up lessons about the Civil War, and I'd wanted to show my students what life was like afterward. Unfortunately, a lot of the Hamilton belongings were destroyed during that time.

"Who are these people to you?" Kylie asked, holding up one of the pictures. "On the back, it says Andrew and Mary Adeline Hamilton."

The photo brought a smile to my face. "I was hoping someone would ask." She handed me the picture, and I held it up for everyone to see. "My grandfather told me the story of these two, right before he died. Andrew Hamilton was a wealthy steel tycoon who took a fancy to my fifth great-grandmother, Mary Adeline."

Kylie raised her hand. "Isn't your name Adeline?"

I laughed. "It is. As you know, my family members are huge history buffs, so I know Mary Adeline was a popular woman in her time. When my grandfather told my mother about her and how much he loved the name, she couldn't wait to use it when she had a daughter of her own." I passed it to a group of students who wanted to look at it. "From what I've been told, Andrew's family didn't approve of Mary Adeline. He was forced to give up his inheritance when he decided to marry her." Gasps erupted around the room.

"What happened after that?" Kylie asked. "Why didn't they want them to get married?"

"She didn't come from wealth, like the Hamiltons. I guess my great-grandfather's parents thought she only wanted him for the money. According to their marriage records, they stayed together for seventy-eight years, and had five children."

"You're not going to catch me giving up my money for a girl," Liam called out, shaking his head. A couple of the girls threw paper balls at him and he laughed. "What? No woman out there's going to want a man who's broke."

I couldn't help but laugh. Walking to the front of the classroom, I turned to address the class. "Money doesn't matter, Liam. It can't buy you love. Speaking of which, did you know that your family, the Blairs, and the Hamiltons have been connected for centuries?"

His eyes widened. "How so? Are you saying we're related?"

"If we are, it's distant," I said. "In my grandfather's belongings, I found a lot of Blairs in the registries. I've tried finding out more, but the Blair family didn't keep up with their history like we have. Although, I'm pretty sure you're part of the original Blairs. My best friend is marrying your cousin this weekend and I know he's one of them."

He snorted and rolled his eyes. "I know. The wedding is all my family is talking about."

The picture of my great-grandparents was handed back to me and I couldn't help but stare at it. Their faces had faded over time, but I could still see them as clear as day, even though the picture was over a century old. They were proof that true love existed.

She glanced at the clock. "All right, class is almost over. Please pass the pictures up front." The class broke into conversation, with some talking to their neighbors about their own family history, and as soon as the pictures were collected, the bell rang. "Have a wonderful winter break, everyone. See you in two weeks."

They all raced out of the classroom, and I breathed a sigh of relief. I loved teaching, but I loved my breaks as well —needed them, really. And Christmas was my favorite time of the year.

Once my desk was straightened, I packed up my things. Before I could walk out the door, my phone beeped with an incoming text from my best friend.

Jessica: I have a surprise for you tonight.

I knew exactly what she was alluding to.

Me: Please don't tell me you're trying to set me up again?

Jessica: He's cute! You'll like him. Besides, don't you want a date for my wedding?

She had a point, but I also didn't want to look desperate. I was thirty and single. It's not like I couldn't get a date on my own. There'd been plenty of men over the years; I'd just never fallen in love with any of them. Releasing a weary sigh, I texted her back.

Me: Fine, I'll meet him. See you at the party tonight.

Made in the USA
Middletown, DE
03 September 2020